T0123525

THE *Cat*

IN THE
COLOSSEUM

THE Cat

IN THE
COLOSSEUM

STORIES AND POEMS

Alan H. Friedman

THE CAT IN THE COLOSSEUM
STORIES AND POEMS

iUniverse books may be ordered through booksellers or by contacting:

iUniverse
1663 Liberty Drive
Bloomington, IN 47403
www.iuniverse.com
1-800-Authors (1-800-288-4677)

ISBN: 978-1-5320-5272-9 (sc)
ISBN: 978-1-5320-5273-6 (e)

Print information available on the last page.

iUniverse rev. date: 10/16/2018

The Tell-Tale Hearse originally appeared in New American Review 9, 1970
War Soup originally appeared in Denver Quarterly, 1987
International Love originally appeared in Hudson Review, 1968
Phenomenology originally appeared in The Little Magazine, 1990
Divorce originally appeared in Other Voices 11, 1989
Pain originally appeared as Paris in Fiction International, 1985
From Hand to Mouth originally appeared in Kansas Quarterly, 1985;
The Anatomy of a Poet originally appeared in Partisan Review, 1965
The Cat in the Colosseum originally appeared in Mademoiselle Magazine, 1954
Willy Nilly originally appeared in New American Review 2, 1968
Prelude to a Glorious Fugue originally appeared in The Paris Review 62, 1975
The Search originally appeared in the Hudson Review, 1968
Garden of Earthly Dilemmas originally appeared in Raritan, 1995
Epithalamion originally appeared in Partisan Review, 1966
Summer '90 originally appeared in Denver Quarterly, 1993

To:
Kate, Gregory, and Alexander

Contents

The Tell-Tale Hearse

In Paris if you can't afford to rent a car, you can pick up a used hearse cheap. I had to get to Rome. I was low on funds. I am not nervous. I paid thirty American dollars for her. Tires worn, motor worn, a gas-burner, but breath-taking. She had that classic French body, squared-away Citroen. Utterly unbruised, elegant with curtains all around. In back in the coffin bed, plenty of room to sleep. Room for two.

Polly was metallic by temperament and profession. "Not in a *hearse*!" she said on Friday night.

"Superstitious?"

I felt her in the dark space. Silence. I felt for her in the silent space. She hissed. "Ghoul! Not in a hearse."

"If we can drive in it by day–" I pointed out. But my fingers in blackness touched metal. The same on Saturday. Traveling south.

So Sunday I tried a hotel. Predictable. Everywhere we'd stopped, everywhere we'd passed, we had caused a fanatic sensation. Our black ceremonious vehicle drew up in front of a small hotel in a small town in Provence. Out we came, travel-weary, through a gaggle of geese and a giggle of girls.

And a goggle of guests. An old woman carrying bread made the sign of the evil eye. Inside we went to register as man and wife, which wasn't strictly true. The bellhop coughed. He nudged the desk clerk who stared past our heads through the doorway and crossed himself, and the elevator boy left his post, walking around us to avoid crossing our path.

Polly rose to the attack.

Metallic Polly, my woman, was in fact a sculptress who preferred to work in welded metal and in the nude–that is, naked, and sculpting herself. As for the pieces she called nudes–well, the one she insisted I had to take (among other heavy items) to Rome in the rear of the hearse weighed 400 pounds and looked like a heartbroken woman who had collided with a rusty meteor. It was titled *Ligeia*. Polly herself was marbly and statuesque- a baroque tension in her muscles, classically heavy breasts and hips, lips, and nostrils flared for trouble and haunted gaping eyes. A hard finish on that girl. Hard to deal with. I couldn't say no about taking her Ligeia, because I'd been sleeping with her in the studio in Paris for four-and-a-half months, gratis. Besides, she had a lavish blowtorch moodiness. "Most French hotels," she said to me in French in front of the clerk who'd crossed himself, "are run by imbeciles and pimps."

The pimps accusation was clearly irrelevant; I told her so. And anyhow, *she* was the irrational one, I told her. Last night and the night before. This led to worse. We had another bad night.

At the border the Italian customs were suspicious of what contraband we might be importing. No hearse had ever entered Italy before. Did we work for a mortician? What was that rusty metal junk heap we had in back. Bridling, Polly assured them it was uranium stolen from the French Atomic Energy Commission. "CIA agents," she confided. The results were predictable. Neither amused nor alarmed but clearly annoyed, they went through everything we owned. "You have no right! Those are my personal things. Hank, tell them…" But what could I do, Citizen Harry versus the Italian customs. Losing control, she blurted to them, "You, you let go!" and tried to grab her sketchpad out of the hands of the nearest guard. Predictable. Seeing her discomfort, they went to the limit, insisting on the right to examine every page of her portfolio; you could see they were out to get her, so every nude she had sketched–those drawings which, I knew, and only I knew, were intimate struggles to conceive herself, private as her thighs, her confessions, or her dreams–were inspected by moustachioed border guards who put on a good show–snickered, tilted their caps, scratched their scalps, and winked . . . Oh they had a fine time.

She walked out and waited in the hearse. Finally we were both sitting up front again. I started the motor. "Gas coupons," she mouthed furiously. I got out and bought gas coupons. By the time I got back in I was exhausted. For one thing it wasn't easy for me, this getting in and out–the seat was immovably fixed, it was set too close to the steering wheel, and I'm not only big, I perspire in the rain and it was raining now. I found myself put in the soggy position of defending the customs police and soon the entire social order. "For the love of God, it's not worth getting excited about."

"Human beings," she said, "are repulsive."

So we entered Italy.

The weather was a solid storm all along the coast. After Genoa it got worse. On a cliffhanging stretch where the curve of the road kept dipping over the right shoulder into the sea, the motor began losing power—one of the cylinders gave up for good. By late afternoon it was pitchblack; we decided to stop somewhere . . . where? Drifts of blown fog would clear for a few seconds and then drop round the hearse again. We rose weakly and slowly into the mountains above La Spezia, the only car on the road, looking for a hotel. We saw nothing except the downpour in the headlights. The heavy chassis rocked under us each time the road wound into the wind.

Finally about eight o' clock, near the summit, a house that looked like a roadside tavern. But not a light. Boarded up? Closed until the summer season? It was on the left. To the right, instead of the usual precipice, was a spot to pull off the road. I inched forward. "Watch out!" Polly hissed, clawing at my arm. The headlights illumined blackness, space, and rain. I pulled the emergency.

As soon as I turned her off, steam poured out of the earth— from under her hood. Overheated. Boiling. Who knows— some part of that damn fog coming up the mountain may have been us. I tried some fancy horn-blowing. Puny sounds, sucked away in the whoosh of the storm. Anybody home? Light. . . light flitted behind a second-story shutter, the shutter was shoved, a head showed, the shutter slammed shut.

We waited. A silence of waterfalls clattering on metal, the roof of the hearse. I ran, she followed. "Yell," she commanded. Soaked, I pounded the door. It opened under my fist.

The man in front of me was no more than five feet tall.

The stubble on his cheeks showed in patches. His skin was paper over every bone–his wrists, the sockets of his eyes, his collar bone. A plucked, starved bird he was. He had just pulled on a pair of pants under his nightshirt. His nightshirt was tobacco-stained. He stood there staring at us, dead silent.

I knew three words in Italian. "Sleep," "eat," "pay." I tried *sleep*, and pillowed my head on my hands. The old man examined us uncertainly, strained to see past us, and his dry eyes pulled narrow. I don't know how he discerned that hearse I the darkness, but for one bad moment it had evidently occurred to him, against his will, that we'd come for *him*. He lowered his lashless lids–his eyes now a couple of dried seeds, each showing through a slit in a pod. Then subtly, his expression altered, widened, corrugated slowly till it was cheerful, his gums smiled unnaturally, there was a hint of strain and exhilaration in his welcome. He disappeared energetically.

"I wish he'd stop all that hopping and smirking," she said.

I could usually tell when it was beginning to happen. She grew feisty, hammer-and-tongs, but her eyes . . . I'd watch for a glimpse beneath their mirror surfaces . . . beneath, they held the intent defiant panic that small creatures of the field show when they realize they've become the prey. Her mind awake saw elements of disorder that the rest of the human race pondered when asleep.

"Face like a death mask," she said. "Notice?"

"He's scared of us," I said.

He came back with a candle–an old-fashioned pan-and-stick. Her shadow appeared overhead, distorted so that her soft lines were skeletal. Again the little man smiled his cracked excessive welcome, as warmly as he could. But the candle flame shivered in a draft, the two halves of his shadow widened and flexed like a shuddering moth, he beckoned her with his rooster fingers, and she backed out. She fled. She vanished through the door. I excused myself and found her in the hearse. I got in to keep dry. I offered a cigarette. She refused.

She said, "I want to go on."

"How far?" I said, pulling out a map.

"Drive."

"Spooked?"

"I'm not staying here tonight."

"You don't trust him?"

Silence.

"He's only old," I said. "Wrinkled."

Rain.

"Want to sleep in the hearse?" I suggested.

Wind.

"Now come back inside," I said. "By tomorrow morning this storm will blow itself out, and when we wake up–"

"How do you know we'll wake up?"

"I know. Because this isn't an Edgar Allan Poe story, it's a goddamn roadside inn in Italy on a clearly mapped coastal route right here in red."

"An inn! Nobody's stayed there for years," she said, "and years. The stinking paint's peeling off the walls like athlete's foot."

I got out under a wall of water, blown forward. I dropped the cigarette, opened the hood, eased the top off the overheating radiator with care, fetched an empty gallon can out of the back, and began scooping up water from the audible flood running down the edge of the road. I poured some in. "Turn her on!" I yelled. I struggled round to the window and yelled in.

"Won't start!" she yelled back.

I slid back in. Tried myself. Nothing doing. The little man appeared, smoking a black root of cigar, wearing a poncho and a black felt hat. Rain poured from the brim. He waded to the back of the hearse and shone a flashlight. Then he was up front, under the hood, bent over, listening to the wheezing of the motor as I made her turn over.

He sloshed up to my window and made intricate motions with his fingers while he spoke. I couldn't understand . . .yes, I could. Sure enough. Spark plugs. They were lovely when I got to them, each sitting in its individual pool of water. I splashed to the back of the hearse, rummaged for an old towel, and ended by trying to dry each damn plug.

Still no use. She turned slowly over and died. It was hopeless.

We retreated to the house. I dried myself with the same towel. I was cold. The old man, still dripping in his long poncho and soggy hat, busied around lighting candles. His wet stubbly jaws and wattled neck gleamed enthusiastically whenever the flames wriggled. "Eat?" he said, bringing his fingers to his now mirthful hole of a mouth.

Polly's animal eyes hunted his face. She sat, inconsolably damp, on a bench in the front room, a sort of coffee shop, cheerless, barren, only one badly chipped marble table and a small counter. "If we sit here long enough," I said, "the heat of the engine will dry the plugs and she'll start." The little man, having wriggled out of his poncho, walked over to us from his puddle and bowed. I don't know why. He was happy. I bowed back.

"There's something on his mind," she said. "What? What's he so hilarious about?" Her suspicious body was bent forward on the bench, her knees in sopped slacks spread wide, her spread elbows resting on her knees, her oppressed face resting on her hands, her back hunched to a question mark, and her bosom concealed by a man's shirt.

He handed us each a candle.

"It's off season," I interpreted, "and he's delighted to have guests." Then I offered the inevitable– "Look, let's stay the night." She nodded, accepting it, but sniffing for trouble.

He signaled us to follow him. We did. Up a twist of stairs.

"And the candles?" she said. "Outside he has a flashlight."

"*Inside* he prefers candles, so what? I don't see–"

"You don't see anything." She pointed: light fixtures in the staircase ceiling, no bulbs. Lamp fixtures in the wall. No bulbs.

"So electricity's expensive way up here," I speculated. "Or the current doesn't get turned on till the season starts. Or the storm blew the lines down. Who knows?"

Along a slope of dank hall to the bedroom.

It was a double bed with rust-red covers. Placed in the center of a big, almost empty room, it looked tiny. The windows and shutters were closed, but the storm had managed to get in somehow. A breeze disturbed the fringes of the covers, and went sliding across our ankles. Polly's teeth, despite her pose of skeptical bravado, began to click and clatter. She clamped them together.

He showed us the bathroom at the other end of the hall. As we went in, candles in hand, the old man, lowering his eyelids, produced the same covert, glistening, subtle look he'd given us before. He closed the door.

Polly tried the door to make sure he hadn't locked us in. "Did you see that?"

"He's never seen a man and woman go into a john together," I translated. "That's all." I was wrong.

Her features drew to their center, focused for a plea. "Would you consider," she said, "sneaking back outside and trying to make it all the way to Florence tonight?"

"Sure," I said. "Only–"

"What?"

"I'd rather make love."

"Make love?" she accused me, But gently. Vaguely recollecting a once familiar possibility.

"That bed," I whispered, "looked cozy." I slid my hand up under her shirt and along her spine. She seemed to roll, she pressed her face to my neck. Then her head was tense against my ear, covering it. The sweep of the storm came through. I heard the muffled storm in a conch shell. "Not in that bed," she said.

"What's wrong with that bed?"

"I couldn't tonight. Not here."

"First it was the hearse," I said.

She began soaping her hands, elbows out–graceful but all her movements discontinuous, distinct. Pushed by an overwound spring. It was going to be one of those nights again, foreign bodies in a foreign bed.

Polly, relax, I thought, ordering her in my thoughts.

But when, holding out candles high, we returned to the bedroom, I suddenly saw things her way.

The bed had grown.

It was now almost three times as tall as when we had left it. I stood still, Polly quivering at my side. The blankets had risen from within as though by a yeast, to a height of some six feet, and the whole bed was glowing hellishly. From the center of the dark room, through the red covers of the bed, came a blurred radiance.

Polly rushed for the door. Alarm spread to my feet. When I caught up with her, she was sitting in the front seat of the hearse.

Wouldn't start. "Push!" she said. There was a gentle, perceptible slope ahead. "Come on!" and she got out.

A strong girl, too, from playing with iron, but it isn't that easy, pushing a hearse. Torrents. Surges of slapping black rain. She shoved from the rear, I shoved from a window, working the wheel, and we got the thing on the road by rocking it, but it took every ounce of strength we had to force it to the exact point where the road began to dip slightly. When it rolled, Polly slipped in through the rear door, me through the front. The engine, dragged forward in gear by gravity, coughed . . . spat . . . fired like a motor boat . . . and refused to start.

The dip ended, Uphill from here in both directions. Morbid, cold, hot, frustrated, stormbound, hopeless, I looked under the hood with my own flashlight, found nothing, kept on looking, and saw it. Under the distributor. A wire, hanging loose. I stood up and yelled to the blast, "Damn son-of-a-bitch pulled a goddamn wire!" Even if she couldn't hear, I was sorry I'd said it; some wires come off by themselves. I reconnected it, fastened the heavy hood, made my way back. She started to the touch now, weak but running. She was still too hot. I could see Polly though the big window between the driver's seat and the coffin bed. She called with relief. "What *was* it?"

"He fixed us"–I said it for friendship's sake–"he made sure we'd stick around." It was possible. Maybe he needed money, guests, company? Still, for all I know I'd pulled the wire loose myself, drying the plugs. But "Mangy little cretin," I brought out, and reiterated the echo to myself. "Mangy son-of-a-bitch cretin."

Hearing me angry, she recuperated. She gurgled with delight. She turned to give a farewell glance to our tavern–and "Good God," she cried, stunned, "he's after us!"

A swift glance at the rearview mirror: I saw the old man coming at us though the rain, stumbling, gesticulating furiously. "Cretin," I repeated, and I put the hearse in gear. We moved, but there wasn't much power. Most of the sparkplugs, still wet or wet all over again, were firing improperly. I tried using the choke, which didn't help. The radiator was still hot, the road was going up, I felt the strain on the engine, I felt like telling her to throw her four-hundred pound *Ligeia* overboard. "Throw that junky metal nude of yours overboard!"

"He's gaining!" she shrieked, and tried. She was so frightened, she actually shoved at it, she tried. She could hardly budge it.

I urged the big ancient unpersuadable hearse forward. It wouldn't pick up speed. It slowed. The hill got steeper. I tried slipping the clutch. If we could get to the top of the rise–I glanced and saw the old man in the mirror, larger than life, maniacally threatening, running for us.

Polly twisted around and covered her eyes with her whole arm. I could see her, she was clearly hysterical. I could see over the rise, we were at the summit. The summit elevation was marked, it was clearly downhill from here to Florence. Suddenly steam raged from beneath the hood, and bursts of vapor rose around us, the hearse struggled barely ahead of the old man, spouting, gushing, billowing through the rain like a dying whale. And in that uproar of fog I heard him screech insanely, "Pay!"

I put on the brakes.

The little man caught the handle of the rear door and wrenched the hearse open. "Pay!" he shouted at Polly viciously, reaching in for her.

I sloshed round back. Pay for what? The old man was crying. Good God! I removed his feeble tendonous wrists from Polly's arm and tried to find her buried face.

We might have gone on. Lucky for us we didn't. I had to find out, and Polly came back with me, exhausted child. Our old man was stern, shaken, forgiving. He took us back.

His fingers on mine were gristle. In the bedroom he lifted one corner of the red covers for me. I looked in squinting, nearly blinded. A wooden frame rested on the bottom sheet. It held the upper sheet and blankets carefully high up. Out and away. For a chilled couple on a stormy night. Set in the wooden frame, dozens of electric bulbs–long rows of incandescence–burned with a fiery dazzle.

Bed warmer. His own invention. From deep in his throat came a proud noise like crickets. We made love that night. There must have been three-thousand watts of light in the bed.

War Soup

Sometime in the early hours of the night someone slipped into the blackness of their bedroom through their open window and moved toward their bed until he was leaning over Dennis, not Meg, and Dennis swung into a frenzy of rage–attack! survive!–he clawed at his eyes to tear the mask from his face and he yelled, "Who's there? Who's there? Get out!" so loud that his own thick-tongued voice woke him up.

Nobody was there, but he found himself on his feet, going for somebody's throat with ten clawing fingers.

"Mom–?" Meg asked in the puzzled, patient tone of someone picking up the phone when the call is a wrong number.

She was in bed, close to her dreams,

"Nothing," he said. "I thought."

"Nn?" Meg asked.

"Nobody," he said.

But he kept peering around the room. He crouched, turning slowly, breathing hard. He had to make sure. That panicky energy wouldn't stop twitching through the muscles of his outstretched forearms and poised calves. He had seen

him. The rooster who had shredded that girl last weekend–
he had been in this room. Two seconds ago, so bodily, so
absolutely there, that Dennis didn't want to give him up.

The hallway was darker than the bedroom.

He managed, without a light, to perform the necessary
maneuvers. Found the bathroom, found the bowl. Raised
the seat with his foot as he always did and hoped he wouldn't
miss. He didn't want to turn a light on.

He felt his way down the stairs, turned left toward the
living room, aimed for the couch, bumped into it, and sat
down on the arm, wondering if this thing was going to hang
around all night again.

At 3:30 a.m. Meg's alarm clock went off. Dennis was still
awake, he had already taken a shower, he was whispering in
Meg's ear before her buzzer buzzed, "Take you mark, get set,
go." Private First Class Meg Nielson got set to go. As always,
she ironed het fatigues. Polished her boots. Put on her hairnet.
Tied on her apron. But now that she was living off-base with
Dennis, she sped to the base in his blue van, to open her
messhall well before dawn,

Dennis didn't mind Meg's early start. He read through an
entire magazine. He fixed himself a breakfast for two. Part
of the day he slept, played tennis and took a second shower.

Hungry? He asked her after she got back in the afternoon
and they went for a swim and made love and noticed it was
nearly twilight. Twilight for them was late. So they pulled
on some clothes and got into his van and went out for a bite.
Dennis drove. It was too hot to walk. With the van it took
only a minute and they were in a diner, a pizza diner on the

edge of Columbus, Georgia, near the Bypass that led to Fort Benning.

Thin crust, 15-inch size? Dennis was concentrating—when out of nowhere Meg started telling him all about "this new dead girl."

"Hold it, okay?" he said, since the death of still another female soldier was the last thing he wanted Private Nielson to be talking about when he was out with her, ordering pizza. He asked her, "Pepperoni or sausage?"

"Pepperoni."

Onion he knew she liked. "Plus mushrooms and sliced tomatoes?" he asked, and she nodded, his finger tapped every ingredient on the menu. "How about we add anchovies?" he said, and he tried to think whether anchovies, so salty, would overpower the mushrooms, because of all the unpalatable subjects you could discuss at dinnertime—such as the cannibalism of freezing families who have to eat eachother's dead flesh raw and so forth—of all such atrocities, the one Dennis disliked hearing about most was the mad-dog butchering of young women. "Plus green olives?"

"Green!" she reproached him. Her eyes were green. Focused light pale-green olives. "With anchovies? *Black* olives."

But Dennis couldn't make up his mind.

He poured a mug of beer from the pitcher. He drank some, and once they had finished putting in their order for a six-ingredient pizza, he listened some. She told him:

"You know *where*? You saw the spot. Tuesday, when you drove in with me in the van. Remember the railroad crossing—where I hang a left and shift into first on account of those bumpy tracks? On the right hand side there's this big crackly patch of tar and gravel? That's where. She was laying right out in the open when I drove by in the dark.

"*You* found her?"

Meg moved her head left and right very slowly so that the pitted olives in the whites of her eyes remained stationary. She said, "I only heard about it."

She poured herself two inches of beer. She tasted. She tried it again. She raised her clear plastic mug to the fluorescent lights in the ceiling to watch how the bubbles rose, and said, "She was out there, she had to be. On account of they said she was found at dawn. And I went past around four a.m. So my brights must have flashed right over her when I slowed for the turn. Thank god I didn't notice the pieces."

Dennis looked around for the waitress. Meg curled the corners of her tired mouth down.

Then she curled up her fingers to have a look at her red-polished nails. "They said she was cut in parts, one whole arm lopped off like the first girl. Half of a leg. Plus different-size pieces sort of dropped in a wiggly line, like she got dumped out of a slow moving car."

"Refugees," Dennis said, "from Vietnam."

"What?"

"They own this diner. They make the pizza."

"So?"

"It wouldn't surprise me if they sprinkled the top of every pizza with 10cc's of *nuoc nam*. Which is full of MSG—the Vietnamese love MSG like the Chinese—I bet you never even heard of Chinese Restaurant Syndrome."

"Quit changing the subject."

"A kind of low-grade paranoia. You can get dizziness,

claustrophobia, some other creepy mental states they haven't got around to classifying yet. This favorite Chinese place of mine in midtown Manhattan? Around Forty-fifth I think it was. I used to go there when I was in dental school whenever I had to knock off the books. I couldn't take one more page, I'd zip out for a late-night snack. I'd always order their War soup. Delicious. They served it in a walloping-big porcelain bowl–and it was a different soup every time. They threw in their leftovers . . . if you came late enough, you got the works. Shrimps, beef, chicken, pork, snowpeas, water chestnuts, and *now* I realize, an overdose of MSG. That's monosodium–"

"Glutamate. I know, and it sounds disgusting." Meg's teeth and her tongue looked like she was tasting the word. "Glutamate."

"If you pronounce it, I agree. Absolutely. But what glutamate did to their leftovers on Forty-fifth Street you would not believe, it was so hypnotic. After my War soup fill-up I started to think every waiter was standing around waiting for me to nod off. The restaurant began closing in on me. I thought I was going to be shanghaied. Right there at the table as I gulped the last of the soup. Or in the men's room if I dared go take a leak. Or just when I stepped out in the street I'd be hit on the head by a Chink. Kidnapped by taxi and carried on board a Chinese freighter docked at the Hudson piers, I tell you, I was a glutenous wreck by the time I finished that War soup. Only it was irresistible, so I kept coming back for more, taking my life in my hands until the day I heard about CRS, that's–"

"Chinese Restaurant Syndrome. Dennis, I got it," She poured more beer for them both. "MSG brings on CRS."

"Right."

"Now will you stop?"

"Stop what? I'm telling you—I read about it. There was this article. Either it was *Science Digest* or the *Journal of Dental Research*. About some chemist, I wouldn't know his name, but he realizes he's suffering from it, from CRS. So he works on it, he researches in his lab for years, testing every ingredient they use in Chinese cookery until he comes up with the exact right one: MSG, which naturally they stir into every dish."

"What kind of beer is this, do you think?" Meg turned around on her bench, looking for their pizza. "What's your point?"

"You're not listening. The point is, I came across that article on CRS and I stopped having symptoms. No dizziness, no claustrophobia, no jitters about slant-eyes waiters getting set to club me. Strange, wouldn't you say? Scientifically speaking? The minute I found out what I go through is ordinary . . . has a name . . . isn't caused by any far-out peculiarity in me—bang! Gone. I went right on eating War soup but all I ever felt after that was sort of hilarious."

"You know," she said, "you're weird."

"I'm not through . . ."

"That's a bitch—you realize you started out with Vietnamese pizza?"

"Of course. Because I couldn't help wondering. Last night, when that butchering took place? Whether there could have been anything. Something. I don't know. I mean something unknown to me—which could have triggered the pains I had."

Dennis touched his belly. "In here."

"You had pains?"

He told her. "It started, I felt this clawing and pecking inside me, like pincers. And afterwards I got out of bed and I couldn't stop thinking–about this Vietnamese surgeon I met in Saigon? Worked in the same hospital with me, and how I met him is, I was eating lunch, I was trying anyhow, hospital food, when all of a sudden he slides his tray over and plunks down next to me. I don't know he's a surgeon. I don't know him from Adam, but it so happens I have a bellyache, only he doesn't know I've got a bellyache, but the next minute he's telling me about some surgical anomaly, some poor slob out of rice paddies, an old guy who kept complaining about atrocious pains in his abdomen till one day they decided to cut him open and they found–oh yes, by God, I swear, Meg–inside him they found a small live rooster. With a beak, wattles, claws. A few feathers. This rooster had been living in his abdomen for years. "No one!"

"Quit it, Dennis. Now! Just quit it." She stood up as if she was going to walk out on him.

"No one on earth knew *why*!"

Meg left for the ladies room and after a while she came back and inspected her fingernails till her pizza arrived, and Dennis said it was thinner and more scrumptious than any damn pizza he had ever gorged himself on.

They drove home from the diner in Dennis's van, sort of rolling downhill to the door of their new apartment and while they were rolling, Meg decided to ask, "Dennis, how long are you going to shilly-shally before you make up your mind about me?"

"About you? Meaning what?"

Meg was offended and she refused to explain. But Dennis knew what she meant, she meant make up his mind about marrying her. "I don't know," he told her. "If it would work. I'm thinking."

"Don't bother," she said. "Don't think around me. Just leave. Split. Go back to Chicago, Go back and rot."

"I won't rot. I go back, I'd still be thinking."

"I'll remember that," she promised. "I'll have it engraved on your headstone. Here likes Dennis Kulick, D.D.S., thinking."

He parked by their front door. "Listen, I gave up my practice to come out here and live with you and try to decide—"

"You didn't *give* it up, you're here on vacation, how long has it been, three weeks? Comes the end of the month it'll be 'Bye-bye Meg, great seeing you again.' You and your dental practice! —what practice? – you only work for a group, and for all I know they just fired you. You worked for a group in Cincinnati, in Seattle, in Chicago . . . anyone ever manage to put up with you even one whole year?"

"My ex."

"Who finally drove herself off of a bridge. Correct?"

Close, that was close enough. Dennis slouched, chewing on his lips.

"Sorry, I didn't mean . . ." She reached over. She doused the van lights. "I wasn't thinking."

"Marriage, it's murder. Meg, I'm telling you."

Meg pushed open the van door but turned to say, "Another thing, I'm sorry you get pains but if you get them again, stay in bed. Don't walk up and down in the middle of the night— you keep waking me up—and damn it, if you absolutely have to go driving around just because you can't sleep, at least when you get back don't take a shower. I need my rest."

The air inside their two-story apartment was sticky-hot. Neither of them had bothered to turn the air conditioning on. Meg headed straight for the stairs and marched to their bedroom.

Dennis had once told her in Chicago—before they'd broken up and Meg had enlisted—that she must have an invisible built-in device, and energy-saving gadget. An automatic three-minute timer with a positive cut-off switch. He used to imagine the location of this switch somewhere near the base of her spine. All day long she could be an internal combustion engine going fullspeed terrific energy buzzing doing accomplishing hard-at-it and then suddenly she'd wind down, she'd go into her three-minute cut-off phase, and soon she'd click off. Out. Not like a lightbulb. More like an engine with vapor-lock. He could keep revving her up, but she'd stall if he tried to move her, she'd just sort of die on him.

"Goodnight," he said to the worn-out soldier who had toppled onto their bed with her eyes closed.

Meg answered, "It's only half a mile from where this second girl was found to–"

"Damn, it's hot."

"From there to the kitchen I work in. And she–"

"No more, okay?"

"Okay. Only–"

"Only what?"

Meg's eyes were still tight shut. "I knew her. Slightly. She was a cook, a new cook, just like me. Dennis I *knew* her. She was in my platoon.

He held her. She was perspiring, flushed. "It won't happen to you," he told her.

He was almost sure about that, and he only had to hold her another minute or so. He tried to take off her unlaced boots but she kicked him. He was pulling the first boot off and she kicked him with her other one. But he got both her boots off and her long hot socks and then, since she was still in her tee-shirt and khaki pants, he decided to turn the air conditioning on.

"Turn it off. Off."

Meg hated air conditioning at night. Dennis turned it off and tried to get the rest of her clothes off but she flailed at him with her arm and he let her lie there, hot, too hot.

He opened the sliding door. The outside air rushed into their bedroom. It wasn't any cooler, but at least it was air that moved. Moved over his scalp, over her neck and arms, neck and arms he could possess, marry, remove, leave, take.

He negotiated the stairs in the dark.

At the back of their place, downstairs in the living room, he unlocked the sliding glass door to the wooden balcony and went out. He stood at the railing and listened to insect noises. The Bypass, he couldn't see it, remained soundless. Except for one car that went hoarsely uphill and away, and then it was soundless again. Overhead, against the hazy glimmer of the nighttime sky, foliage stood out, black, like a two-dimensional cutout, a jungle of edges.

Trying to make up his mind what to do with Meg, he looked into the pooled blackness below. He put both legs up over the railing and he dropped, after judging the distance to the invisible ground, in a crouch, ready to fall forward on his hands. He landed softly, as easily as he had landed last night and the weekend before, and he stood there, listening.

He was alive–grateful to be alive. Intact, awake, only a few feet below their back deck in Georgia. With Meg sleeping above him and not another soul he knew anywhere close, not for hundreds of miles. A semi began to haul its load up the hill. The noise of its laboring engine filled his head while he thought about feeding his rooster a woman's leg severed at the knee. It was hard enough to extract the teeth from a woman. He had this patient once, so young, and her gums were so hopelessly diseased, there wasn't much choice, he took her teeth out, all of them. But a leg or an arm was another matter. An arm removed from the ligaments of the shoulder, torn loose and cut off. The raw flesh, chipped bone, severed muscles gaping out of a casing of blue-gray skin.

The ankle and foot, with the boot still on it.

The wetness of the work.

He pulled himself back up on the balcony, he got a grip.

And with a hop, he hoisted himself over.

He leaned, he rested. His hands tightened on the rail. He rested with his beak thrust out and his wings hunched, trying to decide if it was the right thing to do, marrying Meg.

International Love

Mostly I ate out in Paris, the cheapest places. But the few staples I did buy, I bought in the store just downstairs from me, so two or three times a week I got to talk to the greengrocer. "You didn't know? But yes certainly." My greengrocer's eyes and ears went up together, a child's fat face with a big moustache, and he told me he hated her frothily: standing amidst his lettuce and leeks, into the sawdust he spat freely. I gathered that my landlady Madame Dijour was a rent-gouger. She owned four or five houses in the neighborhood and she was charging me three times the rent I should have been paying. "Miser and pig, ah, she's well-off but you can get nothing from her, not if your wall folds or your ceiling rips. But her husband, ah that was a jewel, a good man, a gentleman, and in this neighborhood, a friend, a leader. Well of course, yes in the Resistance, tortured by the Nazis, killed. God will pay them back what they did to him. But she, the one upstairs, the Queen, he left her all this, and she's worse than the Nazis, you don't know the half, I assure you. The way she treats that little girl of hers, that alone they could hang her for."

I had heard noises downstairs, whimpering noises that I couldn't identify. My landlady had me worried. She was a dyed blonde whose plump face must have become unappetizing somewhere along the line. After I'd heard the story of her husband's torture, I seemed to see it in her face and voice. Each of her eyes had a different shape, sagging and rimmed like two healed cuts on a tree trunk. When she talked to me in her skeptical, twittering French – "Good evening? What time is it. Early for you?" – question marks came out all the wrong places. The idea of going home that night began to make me nervous because she seemed to be lying in wait for me. Regular as clockwork, after an evening of coffee and pernod on the boulevard, I used to start worrying about Jacqueline and her mother. I lived on the top floor. I used to sneak in at the ground floor entrance like a burglar – I'd wait one minute until the timer had turned off all the lights on the stairs – and then I'd tiptoe upstairs, trying to slip past my landlady's door on the first landing. It got so that I was afraid of the door itself – morbidly nervous about the way it had of suddenly snapping partway open . . . because the stairs would squeak, and Madame Dijour would catch me more than half the time. "You're going to bed" – with that chopping innuendo – "Now?"

Her voice was bright, steely. She knew not one word of English. With her French participles she seemed to be snapping her longnailed thumbs; imperatives and subjunctives flashed round me this way and that with a sneer and a controlled hiss. "Turn it so, insert the key softly, incredible hour, I might suggest you remove your shoes *before*." Even matters of information were delivered with hints and barbs – "Rushing in again, no, not you, your countrymen, the news look bad tonight?" And in her simplest phrases something vaguely indecent. "You're going to bed? You're going to sleep? Everything all right?" Not seductive – she'd never invite me in. She'd just begin by complaining about the noise on the stairs, then switch to the international situation, her favorite topic – swaying there in that yellow doorslit of hers in her opaque nightgown at midnight or 1:00 A.M. and asking me if I'd heard the latest news bulletins.

So it wasn't until the afternoon her door suddenly opened wide and she invited me in that I finally got to see what the whimpering noises were all about.

The gendarme in her parlor startled me. "It's all right," my landlady said. "Don't stand there like a donkey. You've done nothing wrong."

As usual I was wrapped in brown burly secondhand clothes. But I felt neither very warm nor well enough concealed. In the dry winter air the points of my hair stood out, disheveled and electric like my thoughts.

"Monsieur," the officer inquired, "Monsieur *what*?" His voice wavered in its pitch, suggesting that my real name could hardly be whatever I was about to claim. I didn't think but I *felt* he had come to arrest me for my thoughts about Jacqueline: he held open menacingly at his waist a thick black book that was chained to his trousers' belt. "Perhaps we can walk upstairs to your apartment?"

"Please, not at all," Madame Dijour insisted. "Stay right here." Jacqueline said nothing. Absorbed in her schoolwork. "You can discuss our affairs here."

I thought of objecting. But the police officer had already

begun writing my answers before he began asking me questions. "Very good, you are a student? You are American? Age, please." He had been oiled: a half-empty bottle and a couple of glasses rested on the table.

There were two animals asleep in the apartment. The pregnant cat I had often seen on the stairs lay curled in a basket; on the chair alongside Jacqueline slept the little dog. "And you have occupied the premises above, renting from Madame Dijour, for three months?" Seated at the smaller table, Jacqueline dipped her drying sunflower face from book to book – evidently translation.

Twice a week for the last three months now I had been giving her lessons in English composition. In fact, when I had first tried to come to terms with her mother about the rent, Madame Dijour had insisted on English lessons for her little girl. These were not a favor, she had explained, not a voluntary matter; they were something I would owe above and beyond my rent. But I didn't regret the arrangement, on account of the little girl's doglike pathos, and something else. I was nineteen, she was fifteen. And when she'd sit at my kitchen table and lean forward to look into my big dictionary, I'd lean too as her skirt rode up, and I'd study the cursive script her blue veins traced on the shaded dry yellow scrolls of her inner thighs. When she'd catch me by glancing up unexpectedly, I always thought I was going to discover from the look in her eyes what went on downstairs at her mother's. I kept thinking about her father. Jacqueline had eyes like faintly tarnished medals earned for unknown acts of heroism, and I looked at their large dry surfaces to discover what willpower, what hand-to-hand combat, what sacrifice, and I learned nothing –or rather something else – that I'd been leaning too far, and that she regarded me with suspicion. After a while she'd go back to work, and while she scribbled, always with many elegant curls of her penmanship, I schemed to take and gently guide that stamen of her pen and the little cluster of her hand over the page so that her ink would flow in flawless English and the angle of my elbow could touch the bell of her breasts. And I did no such thing.

But at night I'd try to imagine what it was that Madame Dijour was doing to her, what it was that left Jacqueline looking like a field of crushed flowers. Over the months my night life in Paris had become a lively and depressing burlesque. Sometimes I imagined Madame Dijour asleep in her warm bed and Jacqueline naked and shivering in a cage fixed into the wide-open window, and I wanted to slip through my window and crawl down the wall and sneak through her window and unlock the cage and cover her icy flesh with my body, but I didn't, because in my fantasy my own window, when I reached it, was stuck, warped and clotted with a luminous mold. Or sometimes as my wits wandered toward sleep I imagined that Madame Dijour had been in the pay of the Nazis and ratted on her husband for whose murder she'd had her own daughter deliberately framed and condemned to serve in the galleys, and Jacqueline there became a kind of Saint Jeanne Valjean, and she was rowing naked and sweating, and I wanted . . . but didn't. So maybe you can imagine what an ordeal it was for me when the gendarme in her mother's parlor quietly asked to see my passport and began checking it against a list he kept in his thick black book.

I had no idea what he was investigating, but I was young

enough so that it actually didn't occur to me to ask. I simply handed over my passport, which I always carried, and said to Jacqueline in slow English, as calm and gay as you please, "Jacqueline, what country am I from?"

She didn't answer. She looked up – yellow skin and yellow-white eyes – sucked her underlip in, and then looked away . . . immobile, suspicious features that would some day be jowled like her mother's but were now just short of ripeness, pale plentiful hair pulled very tight and a thin throbbing throat. For all the yellow blossom of her face and those breasts which were already swaying flowercups, she was skinny everywhere else –stemlike, stalklike, her inflexible arms, her in-folding shoulders, the hardly-any bumps on her hips. But in my mind's eye an older Jacqueline, surprisingly honored at graduation for her progress in English, had been chosen to deliver the valedictory address (her theme, International Love) ; and God ! it was my own tongue-tied Jacqueline, now speaking passionate English stark naked before a thrilled auditorium; and afterwards I tried to rise with a splendid gesture to congratulate my pupil, extending not my hand but, "Your exact rent please? Per month, Monsieur."

Madame Dijour said loudly, "Eighteen hundred francs." She paused, then repeated the figure firmly.

This was one-quarter of the correct amount. So it was she, not I, who was threatened . . . a rent-control check. Was it a mere formality by now? . . . had the cop been bribed? . . . what would my grocer have answered? I saw now why she had always refused to give me rent receipts. But if I called her bluff now, I stood to lose my pupil. Jacqueline translated busily; so I nodded.

"May I see your receipts," the officer asked while writing.

Madame Dijour's eyes arched separately.

Jacqueline with one slow lean arm began to stroke the dog; it stirred. I stirred, the soft stroke on my skin. "I always throw them away."

The officer dipped his head slyly; we were all now in collusion. He finished the rest of his drink. He closed his book and his pen officially, patted Jacqueline's head genially, and closed the door; gone. "It is evident," Madame Dijour said, "that you know how to handle the police." Her mouth was rosy and goldflecked. "And now you will have your reward." You can imagine what I thought.

Her sagging eyes rose to a pointed pause . . . nothing happened . . . and "*Jacqueline*!" Jacqueline rose calmly, obediently, refilled her mother's glass, and filled a clean glass for me.

American students in Paris, the international situation, English composition – we talked about awful things. The first chance I could I said to Jacqueline in English, "How's your homework – easy?" Catching her eye, I tried to wink . . . but it didn't come off, and she only shrugged her thin neck. She motioned for the dog.

"Sss! Poupée!" The dog Poupée stalked obediently past the basket in which the pregnant cat lay dozing, and growled. The cat's eyelids flickered; its jaws opened and it seemed to sigh. Jacqueline caught the dog – it wasn't much bigger than a cat – she scooped it up with a sudden, shy bend and played with its ears. She said in English (startling me), "She is Poupée." (A dirty mop of a dog.) And pointing to the cat, "She is Bijou."

"You see, you *can* speak English," I said. I felt better – gratified to hear her try.

"Jacqueline has never performed very well at school," her mother informed me. "A pity. Mathematics and languages are particular weaknesses, they require the kinds of discipline for which she has no aptitude. But with an American in the house, it is a golden opportunity? And perhaps when the Soviet Occupation comes, she will have occasion to learn Russian – eh, Jacqueline."

It was an odd remark with a suggestion of malice in it – did she suspect something about me and Jacqueline? Did she expect a Russian billet in her apartment? I tried, "You expect war again in the near future?"

"Yes certainly, soon, very soon," she assured me, "though perhaps I will not be in Paris." She drank, then leaned forward and said in her most compelling, mocking tone, "Did you know – how could you know? – listen, at Poitiers in my mother's house I have a vehicle, an automobile, which I keep always stocked with provisions and with a loaded rifle. At the very first signs of trouble between the great powers, of which there have been many during the past years, I have always fled immediately to Poitiers. There at Poitiers I listen continually to the radio. Should there be a more serious sign, I would immediately flee with Jacqueline in the automobile along a route to the Spanish border which I have already planned, to a village in Spain which is already designated. I will not wait this time."

"You really expect to know in advance this time?"

"I don't ever wait to find out. Jacqueline and I and the animals have gone often to Poitiers, eh little beast?" For an instant I thought she meant Jacqueline, but she clicked her fingers and the dog wriggled loose from Jacqueline and came to her at once.

She put it on her lap, saying, "Though of course we shall all be blown to bits by the new bombs, not even Spain will be safe. Tell me, Monsieur, what do you think, are men beasts? Are they capable of reason and foresight? Or will fear make them intelligent – like my little girl here. Have you seen her tricks?" I thought she meant Jacqueline, but with one hand she took the dog by its collar. With her other hand she reached under her own collar, and the nightmare began.

"Please, mother," Jacqueline said, tilting her head.

There was a long pause . . . I cleared my throat . . . "Pastry," her mother said. "Quick." I remember I was sitting in a rocking chair and I began to rock in it nervously. My pupil disappeared into the kitchen and came out again in moments with a plate of pastry. She offered me a piece, offered her mother a piece, then put the plate down near me. Deliberately, she avoided looking at me.

I said, "May I offer Jacqueline some pastry?" I lifted the plate.

"Jacqueline has no desire for pastry, I assure you."

She stood by her mother's chair, a twig of her mother in a short skirt. I wanted to resist . . . though I had no idea yet what I was resisting . . . I said, "How do you know unless you ask her?"

Unruffled, quite sweet, Madame Dijour shook her blonde head, then craned her neck round so that the flesh wrinkled like a braid. "Jacqueline, there, you see, there are some extra pieces of pastry, would you like one?"

Her tone was inviting. There was a split second in which Jacqueline tried to decide which way her mother wanted the tipping situation to right itself. She bent and touched the dog's fur with her lips. "No, mother." She took the dog.

"Give me that dog," Madame Dijour said. The dog was returned. "Eat that." Jacqueline took the plate. It all happened rapidly and was said softly. "Now eat."

Self-conscious, with restraint, Jacqueline began to eat. She kept her medal eyes pinned to her mother.

With the dog on her lap, Madame Dijour took a sewing needle from just under the inside of her elegant lapel and said to me, "Watch. I suspect you have failed so far to appreciate this fine animal." Holding the dog down, she placed the point of the sewing needle against the animal's black snout. She pressed and the dog began to whimper– no squeal, no bark, only a high-pitched faraway complaint. "You see," she continued, "not to cry out, that is the lesson, that is the hard thing." She withdrew the point, the dog wrenched its head, she forced the point again into the snarling snout – the black lips lifted into a snarl, nearly soundless except for the remote whimper.

She said, "You can inquire of my husband."

Jacqueline had stopped eating.

In her basket the cat's tail swept and twitched in an arc against her sleeping body.

The needle approached again. The dog's helpless eyes, already vast and rheumy, opened wider – the pincushion nose could take it no longer – and suddenly the bitch barked. The noise was stunning. Her head jerked sideways, then shot forward, teeth snapping at her mistress's hand. The needle fixed itself in the animal's upper palate, visibly.

The noise – the rapid motion – were instantaneous and repeated. Terrified squealing *with* terrifying barking – the sounds of two separate dogs locked teeth to throat – the jaws bared, another lunge at the needle, and another, and always the teeth closed over the shaft and the point sank into the half-open palate. Until finally no motion, no sound, and Madame Dijour could put the point into the dry snout at will. Poupée remained rigid. There was not even whimpering now, only the redrimmed watching eyes.

"When the Germans were in Paris during the war," she said, "My husband cried out."

At the surge of barking, even Bijou the cat had begun to stretch. She had risen up in her basket on two legs at the sound, then stretched again. Too pregnant to bother, she curled heavily around, meaning to retire perhaps. But she came instead, evidently by long-established habit – many-treated, sagging, and shaking her paws as though wet – to the foot of Madame Dijour's chair. "If he had not cried out," she said.

There was no attempt to finish the phrase. She lowered the dog to the floor.

My pupil's yellowish cheeks were now white, veined over the jaws and red at the bones, as if she were out in the cold. I had begun a strange slow rocking in my chair – with what feelings I don't know – terror? compassion? hatred? – I had ceased to exist, I think, just as if from the very beginning the dog's torment had wiped me out. I don't remember myself there; I just remember It: It whimpering, It rocking, It mouthless, It freezing, It pushing the needle.

On the floor Poupée lay on her back, quite still, even her

eyes still. Obediently, Bijou's left paw shook with that wet motion again, then the cat's bared claws came through their sheaths, and sank with electric viciousness into Poupée's undefended snout. Well trained.

The dog made no sound – in memory I see her staring at me alone, but probably that's only a trick of memory – eyes without a plea in them, without a hope, and paws folded rigidly against her gaunt protruding breastbone. I still see the cat's paw, always the same one, the left, the claws thin and spread like a spider's legs – the strike so fast it can hardly be seen. But felt, yes. And I am rocking faster. The rungs of the chair creak slightly. Besides that, there is only one sound in the room – a whimpering. Not Poupée's of course. Jacqueline's mouth is closed, she is slowly chewing her pastry, the sound comes from there. With all the life left in me I want to rise, to mother her, to marry her, to caress her, to love her. But I don't rise. Her eyes are yellow like Poupée's but smaller, and she is moaning. I hear it still.

Days later we sat through the next lesson in my kitchen, neither of us saying or doing anything out of the ordinary. But when she began as usual to recopy her composition, I took the hand that held her pen in my own hand. She looked at me in a way that seems meant to end the lesson. We kissed. When her tongue came out suddenly to taste mine, I thought she'd be my first French girl, and I took her close . . . but no, she escaped right through the door of my apartment and downstairs in through the door of her mother's apartment.

A couple of days later after that, when I came tiptoeing anxiously up to my place, key in hand, I distinctly heard the cat wailing. The laundry room from which the sound came was opposite my door. I went in cautiously.

My pupil was in there. She seemed excited, skinny, tired – leaning against one wall, her shiny elbows tight against her waist, her flowerbell breasts pressed between her arms. It was a bare room, just the big laundry sink, a bucket and mop, four grey walls and a closet door. I sensed that the two of us must be alone in the house, and I began to have thoughts, concrete thoughts . . . would she feel less afraid of discovery here in the empty laundry room with me . . . or could she be persuaded to come to my bed across the hall? Against the door of the closet the cat Bijou rubbed it back peculiarly.

"Go away," Jacqueline said. "Please." Something had changed. Clearly, I was unwanted. Yet in some way I couldn't fathom, she did somehow seem excited by my arrival . . . and yet exhausted. I went to her and touched the slope of her shoulder. I never touched her again after that. The moment I caressed her, the cat's wail modulated to a new pitch. My movement must have done something – increased Bijou's urgency – the gyrations against the closet door changed to frantic clawing. Her claws audibly tore through the surface of the wood. She must have just had her kittens. – I hadn't noticed any change in her heaviness, as a matter of fact. It was Jacqueline's face I'd read: emptied, sagging with fatigue and joy, as if she'd given birth in pain. I asked, "Did you lock her kittens in the closet?"

She didn't answer.

Slowly horrified at her expression I said, "Did you drown Bijou's kittens?"

Her eyes were fixed on the closet door; she hadn't been

crying. Except for an irregular swallowing, except for an almost imperceptible rubbing of her childlike wrists against her thighs, she was very still, she hadn't moved since I'd come into the room, I doubt if she'd actually looked at me more than an instant. But now – I was startled – she gently pinched my arm. It was slight, but evidently important; she had decided to share something with me. "No," she said finally, "they are alive. Six. Four black kittens and two grey-and-white. I have given them to Poupée."

I thought I hadn't heard correctly. "You gave the kittens … to the dog?"

"Don't be afraid. She wants kittens too, yes, and she will love them as much as Bijou. But I have disciplined Bijou now, which she deserves." She was very happy.

I forgot all about Jacqueline. I tried the closet door. It was locked.

She was on her way downstairs. Had I wanted . . . ? I almost lost my voice. "Jacqueline!" Jacqueline was gone. "Give me the key!" The cat stood on her hind legs, straining for the knob as though to help me – I tried to force the door.

The new noise must have wakened them inside . . . the dog began to bark . . . a piercing maternal yelping sound . . . a bark of triumph . . . and the six newborn blind bits of kitten flesh began to pipe . . . shrill, faint, so many, with such energy . . . the cat went wild at the doorknob– and I heard Jacqueline's terrible loving vengeance, her motherly delight, the dog's brute throat exploding through the wood-work, proclaiming that there was justice on earth, that love followed patience, that after mutilation came six puppies.

Phenomenology

"**W**ho's your French lover?" I demanded before the wedding, trying to discover if she'd had any men other than me since her first husband's death.

"Say that again?" Roxane requested.

I sipped her cloudy Pernod before repeating it, and Roxane put down her drink to scrutinize me before inquiring, "where did that come from?"

I pointed to a framed photograph. It rested on her bookshelf, a memento of her summer abroad; I'd noticed it before.

He was hard not to notice.

Bare chested, without a smile, he was seated astride a motorcycle, perspiring. He had a head that looked like a hardboiled egg. Entirely bald. He couldn't have been much more than 35. So he probably shaved his scalp. No beret–but he was French. He had autographed the photo: *Au revoir,* Claude.

"Oh Claude," she said, crossing her extra long legs.

That's all she said. She tilted her Pernod and water and knocked it back. But what she must have meant, if I now understand the leggy philosopher who became my wife, was that ships and shoes and cockroaches violate the rules of God and man.

A voyage across the Atlantic–expensive, but hang the expense!–I invested the cash proceeds of our wedding in a honeymoon for two aboard an ocean liner bound for France. Lots more romantic, I told Roxane (waving our cabin reservations in front of her two frost-pane eyes) than a quickie trip by plane.

Our ship made the crossing in five days. The hull throbbed, the sky was overcast, the slate-colored sea heaved, the deck leaned toward the waves. Roxane was sick. In the dining room she couldn't eat, in the cocktail lounge she couldn't drink, and she couldn't make love in our cabin.

"Romantic," she said, "my foot," as she threw up in the sink.

She lay back on the lower bunk, wearing the silk nightgown my mother had given her as a wedding present. I stretched out beside her. She moaned, "listen to it throb."

"The ship?"

"Maybe."

I touched her lips with the gentlest kiss possible. She sat right up. She took off the nightgown and tore it from hem to bodice.

I sat up too. She hissed at me, "He didn't."

"Didn't what?"

"Didn't die of a heart attack."

"Who didn't?"

"Who do you think?—my first husband. I lied, I always lie about it, the facts are too sick to put into words."

"Whatever your first husband died of–"

"I'd like to make you sick now too. He died of polio. I don't know if you know this, Percy, but polio's been licked, nobody dies of polio anymore. Except him. And I'm expected to believe it happened? Do I? Do you? He lived for seventeen months inside an iron lung. I made it through fourteen months. Have you ever listened to an iron lung?"

"Pictures–"

"It puffed. It puffed. It puffed. He became an engine and the only thing he could move by himself was his eyes. The last few months of his life I couldn't believe my own eyes."

"Of course you couldn't."

"No, I mean I wouldn't go see him any more. I stopped visiting. Nobody grasped it, none of our friends. I couldn't endure the sight of my husband dying, that's what they said, all of them, doctors, friends, interpreting me to myself, pretending to forgive me, and that was bad enough. The truth is, I didn't believe in that iron lung. Maybe my husband was in there, maybe he wasn't. And now I'm on a ship with you. It has to be meaningless, or if it means anything, what it means is nothing."

Trying to comfort her, I led her up on deck for air. She was weak, she lost her footing. I had to hold on to her arm. "Take another dramamine."

"I'm not seasick." She had her eyes closed. "I'm terrified."

"We're not going to sink."

"I know that, it's something else. Can't you ever

understand?" She clutched at the railing and watched the ocean. "I'm terrified because it isn't there."

"Listen, I think maybe you'd better lie down again."

"It's vast—it's thick," she said, "and it's not there."

The Atlantic was there. I gulped its scent, I took thirsty breaths. I enjoyed inhaling Roxane too. Passionately—everywhere. The strong smell of her scalp when she hadn't washed it for days, the artificial pungency after she shampooed. I sniffed for fluctuations in the odor of her scalp.

The Atlantic was passionate too. Riled by Roxane's denial, it whipped itself up to convince her. It kept right on trying—even when the weather turned sunny.

She groaned, "We could have flown Air France."

The sun broke through the clouds. In the glittering afternoon we sat around in deck chairs. I got out my sketchpad and sketched while Roxane tried to teach me French. How to count from one to ten. Words for bread and water. Roxane gave up, began writing postcards. I got my camera and took pictures. I focused on her and said:

"Who are you writing to now?"

"Your father. To thank him."

"Still nauseous?" I was shooting with the Leica. The deck steward served us camomile tea. The ship rolled left. Wan, waxen, my wife put her cup down on the planks of the deck.

"Don't look now," I said to distract her from her misery while I clicked off a shot of her. "But I think I just spotted the man on the motorcycle."

"Spotted who?"

"Your French friend Claude. Behind you—over there."

His black bikini looked French to me, that's all. He wasn't

bald, he had a full head of hair, he bore no resemblance whatever to the man in Roxane's photograph. This fellow was playing shuffleboard alone, barefoot, not far from the pool. A white shirt, unbuttoned, fluttered from his shoulders. Not a casual shirt, a long sleeved dress shirt—cuffs fastened with cufflinks.

Roxane glanced over her shoulder. "Never saw him before."

I caught her in profile. "Don't try to deny it. You gave him those cufflinks in Paris last summer."

She attempted a smile. "A parting gift. He'll wear them forever. He's so sentimental, he must have flown to New York without telling me—just to catch this ship. That's Claude for you. Follows me everywhere."

Roxane's lips quivered, she closed her eyes while the ships rolled right.

That stranger noticed our attention and came padding over, stick in hand. "Pardon me if I intrude." His musical line in English was French all right. "But will you permit one small hint?" You look quite seasick. Shuffleboard at sea is, how you say—medicinal? Perhaps you shall join me?" He inclined his head.

I asked for his name. Damned if it wasn't another Claude.

"Will you play?" he asked. I declined.

Roxane accepted, sick as she was. She played although the ship rolled, she played although the deck pitched. It went TILT like a giant pinball machine in Claude's favor.

Afterward my wife looked happy.

She had lost every game. I asked her, "How can you lose a shuffleboard match and look so pleased?"

"Claude was right. I don't feel sick anymore. In fact I feel...Percy? Let's go back to our cabin."

Roxane had reserved our hotel room in advance. My philosopher-wife threw the shutters open as wide as possible and gazed out at Paris. "Is it an illusion?"

"It doesn't look like New York." I took pictures through the open window. Chimney-pots on the rooftops below. Steeples in the middle distance. The Eiffel Tower splitting the horizon. "What you see, though, and what I see are two different–"

"Percy, shush, you don't understand the first thing about phenomenology or idealism."

"Don't I?"

She turned, shook her head, smiled. I kissed each cusp of her moist lips, left and right.

We did it right there at the window while I held her on the sill, with Paris behind her.

We did both. First we did phenomenology and then we did idealism.

"I can't see Paris," I chanted as I supped. "It's gone. Bring it back."

She brought it back. I idealized her. If you take idealism seriously on a sill with the window open you may be in for a leap of faith. We didn't fall out; she kept trying to remove my Leica dangling from a strap around my neck. She couldn't wrest it away form me, I wouldn't let her.

"I want your heart," I told her.

"Don't have one."

I raised her sweater and took it anyway. At exactly the right moment. CLICK. Against her chest.

"Don't ever do that again."

Afterward I took a walk alone.

"Hey wait, I'll only be a minute—aren't you going to wait for me?" She was using the bidet.

"Be back in half an hour."

"Percy, I call that rotten."

"Call it what you like." Call it unfocused love, poor setting, faulty speed, insufficient depth of field. Out I went to see what I could see of Paris, by myself.

The one thing I didn't want was my wife's help.

I took to the streets and took pictures. A motorbike parked at the corner. Parisians at an outdoor café. Passersby on the streets. A gargoyle high up on a church—until I had clicked off the last shot on the roll. I glanced at my watch.

And retreated the way I had come,

When I got back Roxane wasn't there. She must have gone out looking for me, so I waited.

The door had been left ajar. That seemed a bit strange— too careless for Roxane. An intruder? A thief? I checked our luggage. Found nothing disturbed or stolen. The key was in the door, on the inside, But I had left it on the dresser. Then I noticed how rumpled, how very mussed, the bedspread was. Under the bed a shoe.

Just one. A man's shoe. Black. Good leather, well polished.

Certainly hadn't been there before. I picked it up. It looked French and it smelled French.

Roxane came back worried. She said, "Where *were* you?"

I showed her the shoe. She couldn't account for it. "Ah

God, that's so funny!" she said, covering her mouth for a good loud giggle. I'd never heard Roxane giggle before. Laugh, yes, but not giggle.

"Funny, nothing—thirty minutes I'm gone, max—and when I get back here this bed looks like a tornado touched down. Or is that a mirage too? You going to tell me I'm hallucinating?"

"Lighten up." More giggling. "It's an improbable event. But it's not heuristic—so don't overinterpret. You found a shoe, not a condom."

"Did he follow you here?"

"Claude?" She was ahead of me. "Which one? The one with the cufflinks on the ship?"

"The baldheaded one on the motorcycle." Actually, I wasn't sure which one. Either could have found her. It was Roxane who had reserved our hotel: she might have written to one, whispered to the other.

She said, "The games you play in your mind! Listen to this sequence, would you? A rumpled bedspread. A missing wife. A key in the door. A shoe on the floor. And BINGO! Claude?"

"This shoe is real," I said. "Smell it."

"I can smell your suspicions from here."

I put the key in my pocket. I put a new film cassette in my camera and I took a shot of that shoe.

"Oh, great incriminating evidence. Percy, open your eyes. Nothing makes sense—why should a shoe? But I'll tell you what I think." Her blue-frosted eyes fluttered. "First, you leave in a huff. Second, I dash after you. Third, the concierge rents our room to a hooker for a quick trick."

"Clever," I said, "I don't believe it."

"Go on down and ask him."

"Fine. I will."

"Naturally, he'll deny it."

Naturally. "Okay, let's drop it."

"Halleluia. Then come on, how about we take a walk together? I want to show you the Boul Mich. And the Pont Neuf! Last summer, God, I adored that bridge."

We fought our way down to the Seine. Through the crowds, the noise, the odors of the Boulevard Saint Michel. Past secondhand bookshops and stationers and art supply stores. Roxane bought a lemon-colored notebook to keep a journal in. With pages of graph paper—to chart our progress?

I took a chance on a portable easel of very fragile wood.

Tobacconists and corner cafes. French matches, a *sandwich jambon,* and two shots of Pernod. Sidewalks clotted with sharp-jawed, thin-whiskered students from the Sorbonne. I saw jackals and wildebeest. God only knows what Roxane saw. Neo-exstentialists? I aimed my lens at pedestrians and motorists. The traffic was heavy, the air foul. I sniffed it: French fumes smell different from American exhaust.

She came to a halt. She had just caught sight of the bridge. She wouldn't move. "There it is!" she told me. She admitted it. She was damn near ready to weep, she was so overwhelmed. I stood beside her, jealous. She made love to the Pont Neuf with all her heart.

We moved two weeks after we arrived, out of our cheap hotel and into a small apartment. It was off the Rue Fleurus, furnished, convenient, much too expensive. More expensive than the hotel. We figured we'd be saving on meals by cooking at home. It didn't work out that way. Sometimes we cooked. More often we ate out.

After dinner she went her way, I went mine. She was accustomed to independence. So was I. And week by week I saw less and less of her. I tried to tune into my philosopher-wife. Couldn't seem to get the right wavelength.

In general I knew what she was up to. Lots of research for her thesis. Roxane had come to Paris for more than our honeymoon. Classes at the Sorbonne in the morning. Afternoons in museums and libraries. At night she took courses at the Institute of Oriental Art. October afternoons I even attended a couple of her philosophy lectures. I understood nothing. I doodled. On the inside cover of her loose leaf binder I did the professor's balding head and beetling upper lip. . .until Roxane turned over the first page. . .I drowsed off.

My own plan in Paris was to paint, paint, paint. But I spent my mornings in bed, my afternoons sketching Parisians. And I took photographs. Faces, footwear, motorcycles. . .

I was shooting in black-and-white. One afternoon I located a photo supply shop and bought basic equipment and chemicals.

Roxane woke up that night and she wanted to know, "What the hell's that stench? It reeks in here."

The negative of the shoe revealed nothing, but my portraits of Parisians looked ominous with knowing smiles. I studied my street scenes, hoping for a figure with only one shoe. My negative of Roxane's heart, well, that was crystal clear. My lens had been pressed against her breastbone.

One morning a little before noon, I took the negative to a nearby camera shop. The clerk spoke excellent English but he objected, why would I want an enlargement of a totally blank negative? I paid in advance—and asked for an enlargement of the odd shoe.

A Saturday morning, I'm sure it was, because Roxanne hadn't left for school when I left for the camera shop. She had finished plucking her eyebrows and was mending a flannel nightgown—we'd torn it the night before—I kissed her goodbye and suggested a picnic lunch in the Luxembourg Gardens, and maybe she heard me, maybe she didn't.

I stopped to get picnic supplies, using my finger to point. Bread, pastry, assorted delicacies, and I took the stairs to our apartment. Found her back in bed. In her nightgown. I had never before raised my voice to Roxane. I yelled, "Am I daydreaming?" I pointed to it under the bed. "What's that?"

"What?"

"This!"

I lifted it to eye level, holding it by one lace.

She sat up insisting, "Either you put that freaky shoe there or it comes and goes by itself."

"Black, good leather, just like the other one—Roxanne, please tell me very calmly. What's going on?"

She wasn't calm either. "You know what's going on. You brought that thing here from the hotel."

I swung it by its lace. Left, right.

The same size? I couldn't tell. The very same shoe?

Could I have done what she'd suggested, brought it with me from our hotel room—unconsciously? Or could Roxanne have gone to the trouble back at that hotel, of concealing it in her suitcases and smuggling it into this apartment? To mock me? To drive me up the wall and right out of my tree? Wait, this shoe was left, hadn't it first been a right? The shot I'd taken would show which foot—but what difference would that make?

"Your Claude's pretty careless," I said.

"*My* Claude? Stop swinging that thing."

"Either careless or diabolical."

"*You're* diabolical." She gave me a stare as hard as a kick. "And *my* Claude's not careless, he's clean. He dropped by to do his laundry. Take a look in the bidet—he left his underwear in there to soak."

I let go of the lace, the shoe dropped. I took three shots of it from three different angles. What for? I put the camera down, tossed the stinking shoe out the window.

Roxanne jumped up. She made a grab for the Leica, tried to heave it out after the shoe, I deflected her arm, the camera hit the drapes, it landed near a chair, and Roxanne made a dive for it.

I rescued the camera. Did what I could to appease her. I opened the camera case. Exposed the entire roll. Dropped my film into the wastebasket.

Weary, we sat down together in the middle of our bedroom and begun unpacking the supplies I had brought. We picnicked right there. On the floor.

I said, "I bought olives."

"With worms?"

"Probably."

I offered her an olive.

She wouldn't take it.

I had no appetite for food, I browsed on her flesh.

"Cut it out. Not now! You're impossible, quit that, damn

it. Let's just eat," she said. I raised my head from between her legs.

She unwrapped the cheese. I concentrated on the Port Salut, which reminded my nose of the shoe. The evidence was out the window but not out of my mind. If my wife had nothing to do with the shoe's comings and goings, its appearance and reappearance were irrational events. On the other hand—on the other hand, I wanted her more than ever. I couldn't bear to contemplate how much.

She muttered, "You'd better get a grip on yourself." Then came a cry from her heart. I was positive she had one. "Because I tell you. I think we made a mistake." The smile she gave me was bleak. She added, "Open the wine, okay?"

I screwed the cork out of the bottle and took the first swig of wine.

She tried an olive.

I got out my pocketknife. I cut the bread in two, then cut it into slices. And I found, embedded in the loaf, a well baked cockroach, neatly halved by my blade. Its thorax and jaws in one slice. Its abdomen in another.

Roxane, my wife Roxane, my philosopher Roxane, Roxane guzzling wine, was too busy to notice the bread or what was in it. "I hate to tell you this," she was saying. "Even if you didn't plant that shoe, you're causing it to appear."

"Out of thin air?" I spread *pâté de foie* and handed her her slice.

"What a crunch!" she murmured, brushing flakes of crust from the bodice of her nightgown. "Why can't we do French bread this well back in the States?"

I picked up Roxane's heart. The shoe too. Both these enlargements, shoe and heart, were larger than life. When I got home I tacked them to the kitchen wall.

Roxane, coming home late from Oriental Art, ignored the blow-up of the shoe. The second enlargement mesmerized her. She prodded the ridge between her eyebrows. She pulled up a chair and sat perfectly still in front of it. Glossy and black. Resplendent black nothing. Nothing to see. For damn near five minutes she inspected this blow-up without a word. Then she said, "You've caught something."

"No kidding. What?"

"Nothing. Which contains everything–could you paint that?"

"Of course. But it's been done before."

"Nothing has been done before. There isn't any past. So there's nothing to repeat."

"Wrong. I can photograph, paint, even alter the past."

"Sorry, you can only alter your illusions of the past."

"I have no illusions," I said. She smiled to oblige me. But when she got to her feet I asked her, "Roxane? What goes on at the Institute of Oriental Art? They turning you into a Hindu?"

"Sort of." She gave me a sort of kiss, intended to change the subject.

"What time does your last class let out?"

"All right, Percy. Here." She produced from her pocket a small white business card. It was printed in French. She translated it to me. The Friends of Krishna. Underneath that, someone had written his name in ink:

Claude.

Can't say I was surprised. "Claude which?"

"You know which." He's a member of the Friends of Krishna. He rides a motorcycle. I'm taking motorcycle lessons."

"You're what?"

"That's what I'm studying. After class."

"With Claude. At night. Motorcycle lessons."

"Not every night."

"Not every–hold it. Wait. Are you–come on, what the hell's going on? Does he practice mental magic? Does he teleport shoes under beds? Are you making it with a French fakir?"

She replied as serene as Buddha, "We need a motorcycle."

"You're out of your mind."

"You're not?"

Her journal, that lemon notebook she'd bought, was a temptation. In the morning after she drifted off to class I got out of bed and picked it up. I wasn't sure I wasn't *supposed* to read it; she left it lying around.

I found *One-pointed balance. Lost it today. Perhaps when one rides at a roar through so much darkness to reach the light, the fear of falling off, or perhaps merely the noise, shatters the nerves and robs the ride of its full illumination.*

I studied the two enlargements on the wall while grinding coffee for my breakfast.

Morning and night for the next few days I kept busy. I trotted around Paris taking shots of motorcycles. I shot them from angles that enhanced their menace. I bought trays, got hold of a used enlarger. An antique, but it served the purpose.

When my enlargements were ready, I browned their edges by heating them with a clothes iron till they peeled, then I used the ironing board to cement my photographs edge to edge. I mounted them in pairs, curled and burned. I mounted them by the dozen crumpled and scratched. A checkerboard of motorbikes, a frieze of motorbikes, a cross of motorbikes. Roxane came home one evening to find our bed surrounded by motorcycles, a metallic sheen of cylinders, shafts, and wheels. She reclined on our bed with her head propped up on a translation of the Hindu Vedas. I waited. Not a word. . .not one word. She opened Sartre and started reading. In French— with an occasional glance in English at me.

Hungry, I considered making us dinner. Too angry, I polished my boots instead. About the time I finished, she joined me in the kitchen. She sat at our kitchen table and began typing on her portable.

I interrupted her hunting-and-pecking noise. "Give it to me in a nutshell."

"My thesis? I'm not ready for the nutshell summary. But okay, I'll give it a try. To begin with, the axiom of Eastern religious thought is that Being *interrupts* Essence."

"Am I allowed to interrupt?"

"No. Just listen. Creating yourself is the hardest, most important work. That's the Western view. The Oriental view is that it's harder, and more vital, to lose yourself."

"I'm already lost. Roxane, tell me this," I asked—"which way do you lean?"

"I'm Western, so I go for the Eastern view. For balance."

"Ah, balance. I see, and does he hold you or do you hold him?"

She typed a couple of words before saying, "With Claude and me, if there's one thing you don't have to worry about, it's our bodies."

"Reassuring. Quit your typing," I said. "Talk!"

"Be careful how *you* talk," she warned me. "Because so far Claude doesn't exist. Neither the first Claude nor the shoe, neither the second Claude nor the second shoe. My French lover is your misperception—an illusion—and like the rest of your illusions, it's a cheap shot."

I had the feeling if I so much as opened my mouth I was going to make a fool of myself, intellectually, sexually. But East vs. West, plus the Friends of Krishna in Paris, France, together with motorbikes of all nationalities, struck me as a grand shuck. I blurted, "One-pointed balance my ass. Next time you have this fear you're falling off, just zip right over here and the two of you can balance in this bedroom to your heart's—"

"Misreadings are dangerous." She stood up, eyes flickering. "Misconceptions create. Space and time and people create each other. If you empty your mind, Percy, you can step aside."

My stomach growled at her. "I'm famished. Step aside."

This metaphysical quarrel took place in our kitchen at eleven p.m. I broiled us a couple of chops.

I took the Metro to Roxane's night school. I stationed myself outside her friendly Krishna society, across from the façade of the Institute of Oriental Art.

For a quarter of an hour I hid in the shadow of a wall, next door to a neighborhood café. It had outdoor tables even on chilly evenings. Curiosity kept me warm; and my eyes fixed on the doorway opposite. Once my attention wandered to the customers at the outdoor tables—and there, in a wire-backed chair, sat Roxane. She must have been sitting there all that time. Listening. Talking. Her plaid mackinaw was buttoned up against the chill.

Both her eyes had yellow splinters in the yellow light.

Claude had his back to me. His thick short motorcycle jacket, with its knitted collar, gave him a preposterous shape: his lower extremities and hips small, his shoulders fat, no visible neck. The bald oval of his head nested deep in his collar. Under the table, on the seat of a third chair, sat his white protective helmet.

I turned to notice for the first time, wedged between two cars at the curb, a not very impressive motorcycle.

Didn't make a scene. Took the Metro home and waited up for Roxane. Even rustled us up a late-night snack, which I served when she got back. After she had eaten it, late as it was, I insisted that she pose for me, seated in her chair at our kitchen table. I drew her a picture, worth a thousand words. I drew the table. The dishes. Our two empty wineglasses. The bit of meat she had left over. Her chair too. Roxane wasn't on it.

Divorce

My lawyer tells me he's planning to get married, would I brighten his teeth for him? So I brighten his teeth for him, I realign his incisors, I cement a loose crown, and he invites me to his wedding.

It's Sunday morning. I'm just getting over my ex-girlfriend who told me last month, "Bob, you're dead inside, this relationship is not going anywhere, I look at you I see death." Worse, at my age it's worse than losing a woman, I'm still reeling from the blow of getting a week's notice yesterday, Saturday, from who? My dental assistant. She's jumping ship, this rat. But today the sun has burned the fog off the hills and I'm driving to my lawyer's wedding in my white Porsche. At the entrance ramp to the freeway I stop to pick up a hitchhiker.

She doesn't belong out there. She's wearing an ankle-length gown with a high collar, puffed sleeves, lace at her throat, brocaded material the color of pale tea, and in her hand a rosebud. A tea rose. She's hitchhiking with that, not with her thumb. After she gets in I tell her, take a bus, don't hitchhike, how old are you, sixteen? Seventeen? I've got a son—older than you–Noah, he lives with his mother in Chicago–what's your name?

"Cammie."

"Camila? Camille?"

"Cammie."

On her lap Cammie cradles a large brown paper sack. Paper bags, we used to call them back East. What's in the bag, I ask. Her costume, she says. (She's wearing her costume, I'm thinking.) She's on her way to rehearse at the Renaissance Faire in Marin County, would I like to come watch her rehearse?

"Can't. My lawyer's wedding. Got to show up." I'm wearing a tuxedo. "Like to come watch a wedding instead?"

Can't, she says. Could I drop her off please in San Francisco? She'll catch another ride from there.

She will. No doubt.

Some teeth she's got! What enamel! A Class One bite. She's had orthodontia, it looks like from where I'm sitting. I ask, "Where's your retainer?" –it isn't in her mouth–"in that pouch?" I've guessed right. A leather pouch dangles from her wrist. Beaded and tasseled and sewn together out of green pink brown and purple patches. With a bell that tinkles.

"Who's your orthodontist?" I ask. She tells me. I know him: fellow I often use for referrals, Caldwell on Solano Ave. I want to take a good look in her mouth. You can't while driving. I drive her out of her way, to Union Square in San Francisco, where I park illegally, ask her to wait in the car a minute, I've got an errand to run. I run into a florist shop. And come out with a bunch of longstemmed roses. Red. Off the rack–the biggest bunch in the store, ready to go. Twenty-one roses. I give them to her. "For me? Why?" How can I tell her? I tell her anyway. "For your teeth. You should wear your retainer," I add to distract her. "All the time."

I don't mention I'm a dentist.

The whole truth I can't tell her. It's her age. Not her youngness—never mind the pastel glow in her cheeks—I'm talking age. I try, each time I look at her hands, not to let on how shocked I am. The palms and fingers are ancient. Wrinkled. Papyrus palms. A movie, I watched once when I was very small and thrillable, in Brooklyn, it was called SHE—and in it I saw this beautiful woman wither into crone, in seconds, it was terrible. As her skin decayed, my own skin crawled. I never got over it. Two thousand years old.

She reminds me of SHE. I buy her those roses.

I take her to the Renaissance Faire—I don't go to my lawyer's wedding. She's a belly dancer. She's got her belly-dancing costume in the brown paper sack, also her jeans and whatnot else. I haven't got around to installing a phone in the Porsche yet, but I place an urgent call to my son, I put the call through in my mind. The connection's staticky. "That you, Noah?" "Dad, what's up?" "This girl." "Who?" "Cammie. Not even your age." "So big deal." "Noah, pay attention. Belly dancer. Roses. Come August, I'll hit forty-six, and what about my lawyer's wedding?" "Dad, why are you all of a sudden handing me these decisions?"

I hang up.

I'm speeding high on the Golden Gate, saying to my papyrus-palmed hitchhiker, "Some luck you've got. A single ride from Berkeley to the Renaissance Faire."

Luck? she says and sniffs her roses.

We get to the Faire, she goes off to change for her rehearsal, there's no audience except for me. I linger, watching a troupe of dancers rehearse on a wooden stage outdoors. Finally SHE comes out on the boards in her belly dancing get-up and tries gyrating on three overturned shot glasses while sliding all three of them underfoot across the stage. She switches her feet from glass to glass. I watch her, she slips, she hops back up, the crowd applauds. I'm the crowd. Coins are flashing on her hips, she looks maybe five-foot-seven, not much belly, not much hips, skinny in her Middle East costume.

Her rehearsal's over. She gets back in my Porsche and I just can't resist. "Your retainer," I say. "Oh," she says and fishes in her leather pouch. She finds it, slips it into her mouth. "Let's see." "My retainer? What for?" "Let's have a look. Open wide."

Tilting her head, she opens wide. I look into her mouth. I look in her mouth and see something that isn't in there. I see the well-lighted interior of a subway car.

Panic seizes my throat. A New York subway car, I recognize it. I can also see, absolutely distinctly, the ridges of her retainer, her grooved tongue and healthy gums, her glottis and uvula, her even teeth and the bright wire that encircles them. Teeth do not look like passengers standing in a subway car, not even like passengers sitting in a row. The passengers in that crowded car are swaying in unison, they're reading newspapers, they're wearing raincoats and hats, some of them hold umbrellas, some of them are gripping the vertical bars in the center of the car, and then all of a sudden their swaying and rocking movements stop. Their subway train comes to a halt. Their faces turn deliberately, slyly, all of them, and they stare at me.

The girl closes her mouth, the subway car darkens as

though its lights have been shut off, and even then in that dim train I can still make out a dozen shadowed faces and a couple dozen eyes like pen lights, sharp. At the same time I can see the puzzled expression of the girl in my automobile, the Renaissance gown she's put on again, the half-open window behind her, the nearly vacant parking lot, the bushes, the stunted trees, the dusty paths of the fairgrounds.

I get out of my car, I want to get away from her, but I grab hold of the car door, I can't use my feet, they're paralyzed. My hitchhiker comes around to where I'm clinging with both hands to the open door of my Porsche. "What's wrong?"

My voice says, "Can you drive?" Is my speech slurred, is my bottom lip drooping–a stroke, did I just have a stroke?

"You look terrible."

"A dizzy spell." I'm shaking still. "I better not try driving right now."

She takes the wheel, has a learner's permit, knows the way back, takes a series of turns that bring us out onto 101, heading south, while terrible words go roaring through my head. Maniac. Delusion. Psychotic episode. Those passengers–I saw them the way a psycho sees devils. Or whatever it is those crazies see–those crazies don't think they're crazy, other people do. Right now the important thing, got to look for objective signs. Like finding the trace of an abscess on a periapical x-ray, take an outsider's view of my seizure. Little signs. Oncoming breakdown. Anyone, hinting I've been growing bizarre?

Who'd notice? On the West Coast? A skillful professional, that's how abnormal I am, but I'm glaring at the road. Cars glare back at me. I want to say something to the kid who's driving, something brief. Spoken with authority, to prove I'm stable. But a crowded subway car in the mouth of a fetching teenager?

We're passing San Quentin when it takes me by storm, spectacular–Noah. The boy and I–we'd ridden CTA and IRT trains often enough in Chicago and New York–and once we'd had a lousy quarrel on the subway. He told me I was tearing him and his mother "to shreds and pieces." Told me his mother wanted out–my *son* told me. The train was pulling into the station, he tried to drag me to the door in the middle of the car and I shoved him out on the platform; he screamed when the door closed between us.

"Talk. This is a boring bridge."

The San Rafael Bridge. My driver's taking the short route back.

"Don't feel up to it. You talk."

"Okay. I like driving your car. My mom's going to give me hers when she gets herself another one. She's thinking of buying a Volvo. If she doesn't renige I'm going to get her old green Bug."

"Renege," I say, although there's a ringing in my ears, it won't stop, and I pick it up and my ex-wife Sondra's voice says, "Jake, they'll lock you up," and I drop the phone.

"Though what she's going to do with a brand-new Volvo on a Buddhist commune I don't know. What did you see when you were looking in my mouth?"

What am I supposed to say, an impacted subway car, and hand her my card? I don't say anything except for giving her directions when we get across the bridge onto 17.

She asks, "You live in the hills?" "Up by Tilden Park." "We

live in the flatlands, just off of Dwight–what did you see? You looked inside and saw something funny."

Your retainer, I considered saying, looked like it could use a little adjusting, better go see Caldwell.

"Tell me." "I saw a two-thousand-year-old spook in a very young body." "You don't know anything about bodies. Or spooks." Spooks I don't want to listen to.

"Bodies," she lectures me, "are cages for birds."

"So what do you eat for dinner, alfalfa sprouts?"

"Mung bean sprouts." She parks my car and comes around to open the door and give me a hand. I'm staggering. I better lie down. No more bouquets for hitchhikers. "You sure you're all right now?"

"Never felt better. Thanks for driving."

"Thank you. Never before in my whole life has anyone boughten me this many roses."

"Goodbye," I say.

A steep flight down. Fifty-two redwood steps from my mailbox on the road to my house in the canyon. I wobble past my ginko tree, past my medlar, past a peewee lime and unlock my front door. Overhead–something catches my eye–a movement. I gaze up into a eucalyptus tree. All those strips of peeling bark, all those rusty leaves. I can't place exactly what it is I'm staring at, at first. Then I notice two outsize paws. High up . . . a lynx? A wildcat of some kind. No ordinary cat, too enormous for that. Its front legs look boneless. Tentacles, reaching downward along the bark the way a pair of snakes would glide, each leg slinking lower.

This time I don't worry I'm going off the deep end. My house sits on the edge of a wooded park, it sprawls for I wouldn't know how many miles of ridges and reservoirs, which bring me hit-and-run deer, they munch my best plants. Big-eared does, rabbit-nerved stags. Raccoons, skunks.

Still, a wildcat! This is a first.

So I use my key, close my door solidly, hang up my tuxedo jacket, take off my tie, head for the living room and I'm not surprised to find her on my couch.

She's knitting . . . in her brocaded ankle-length gown . . . and doesn't bother to glance up. Lights are burning in all the back rooms, in the kitchen, in the bathroom. How long have I been standing outside? Long enough . . . she's taken a good look around. Must have come in through the patio, through those sliding doors, did I forget to lock them? She slips off her sandals, she wiggles her toes, her ragged toenails make me want to tell her, "Just what the hell do you think you're doing in my house?" but this wouldn't exactly be fair after she's driven me home, so I say the next worst thing, "Hi there Cammie," in the cheery voice I put on to welcome kids into the operatory and I can hear myself going, now this won't hurt a bit. "By any chance you didn't happen to notice an animal that looked like a lynx in my–"

"That was a bobcat," she interrupts with a pull on her yarn. "You know, it's kind of insulting–how you keep on not recognizing me."

Spooks again?

Above her head runs a single bookshelf. It's bracketed to the wall. No books on it now because once, when I kept it loaded with books, this fifteen-foot board leaped off its brackets in the night. No, I don't believe in poltergeists but I was astounded, I admit, by the agility of a bookshelf. *The*

Story of Civilization by Will and Ariel Durant in thirteen volumes, the complete works of Mark Twain, plus nineteen bound volumes of the *Journal of Dental Research*, this heavy shelf did not simply collapse buckle or split. It jumped off the wall. Vaulted over a standing lamp without knocking it down and threw my library across the room. Underneath the same couch on which this belly dancer is sitting, one morning winged ants, termites, swarmed up out of the floor, must have been a thousand, roaming, crawling, unable to fly yet, I vacuumed hysterically, sucked them in by the hundreds.

I want SHE off that couch. I don't want her in this house.

"We'll take you home now, Cammie."

She doesn't stop knitting–something purplish. Her long needles are purple and her fingers crinkly. "My mom," she said, "is a patient of yours. Yvette Hubbard?"

I remember Yvette. I saw her yesterday, Saturday morning, nine o'clock appointment, I remember her partials, lower left dentures.

"You're Yvette Hubbard's daughter?"

"You used to do *my* teeth, too," she says, her lips compressed with resentment of not being remembered by her old dentist. "Until you sent me to Doctor Caldwell to get braces when I was twelve." She knits for two more seconds before telling me, "I thought, when you bought me those roses, I thought, he *does* remember me! I kept on waiting for you to say, 'Cammie, you've changed since you were a kid.'"

She's had time to arrange her roses in a tall porcelain vase I keep my firetools in. My firetools she's thrown into the fireplace. I get my car keys and I say, "Let's go. You can take your roses home in my vase."

"I'm not going anywhere. Whenever you move you jerk and your head's on crooked." She examines me with green-eyed concern. "That was a mild coronary you had before, wasn't it?"

"No, not even a mild one, I keep myself physically fit," I'm bragging to this slip of a girl. "Three times a week I do the Royal Canadian Air Force workout. What do you do for exercise–float?"

"Fly. But only once a month."

"On drugs?" I don't doubt it. "Speed?"

"Be serious, please. I belong to a coven."

"Witches?" What next? Christ, hitchhikers. But I back up a step.

"I'm also a cleaning-lady. Two times a week." She folds her knitting. "A house in Piedmont, fourteen-rooms. I do the bathrooms and the laundry and the windows. I make the beds, I clean and wash. I scrub pots and polish the silver and dust and vacuum and mop and wax–"

"Which is ruining your hands."

"My monkey hands?" she blows on her palms. "I was born with these. Do you know why we're in separate bodies?"

"Who?" I retreat one more step.

"You shouldn't be alone. Not yet." She jams her knitting, long needles and all, into her paper sack. "So I'm spending the night with you."

I find Hubbard, Yvette, in the phone book.

The puffed sleeves of my hitchhiker's Renaissance gown have gotten slightly crushed. She fusses with them while I dial. The line buzzes, it's busy, she's saying. "Working in other people's mouths all day long has got to be absolutely disgusting. You need help, you need nutrition."

"What?"

She stands up, barefoot. At least she's off my couch. "I'll fix you a milkshake with carrots."

She advances on my kitchen. "You stay right where you are." I try to stop her. We collide.

In that instant I see—as visible as the fresh complexion of the kid in my living room—another face superimposed on hers.

I see a rainy street illuminated by passing headlights and lighted store windows. I see the face of a bag lady with hairy cheeks to which raindrops are clinging, two yellow and bloodshot eyes, a torn woolen hat pulled low over her ears, a beat-up overcoat buttoned only at her throat, two stuffed shopping bags dragging at her arms, a woman shuffling like a zombie along a wet pavement, against whose shoulders and chest I bump with an impact that shocks me while Cammie grabs my arm.

I nearly topple over—the wind knocked out of me—though we've bumped only lightly. The bristly face of the bag lady vanishes. But the rainy street remains. Then dims, winks out, is gone. I regain my breath, sucking for air.

Cammie—half-shoving, half supporting me—gets me to stumble into my bedroom, where she lowers me onto the bed and begins unlacing my shoes and pulling off my pants. I try to sit up but she's a no-nonsense nurse. "No," she says forcing my shoulders back down. "you're not driving me home. Not in your state.' She pushes her mouth against my forehead. "You don't have a fever, at least I don't think."

I don't want to sound like a nut but I have to say it. "When people, Cammie, when people look at you do they see . . . peculiar things?"

"They see what they want to see. Because I'm nothing, that's how it works, but I'm going to bed now. In the morning you can drive me to work."

"Hand me the phone," I order.

My bedroom phone is fire-engine red. I dial, lying down, I'm thankful to hear it ringing, thankful when her mother answers. I get a grip on the receiver. On myself. "Mrs. Hubbard, good evening. This is your dentist."

"Doctor Morton? Did I forget to make my follow-up appointment?"

"I'm calling about your daughter Cammie."

"My Cammie? –she goes to Doctor Cald–"

"Right now she's alone with me here, at my house."

"At your house–oh, are you a member of her coven? Her warlock? You? How nice!"

I drop formality. "Yvette, she wants to spend the night with me."

Yvette Hubbard says, "Yes? Oh, I see. Well, it is short notice," she sighs. "I'm expecting company. Though if you need any help controlling her I could drive by and take her off your hands."

Cammie grabs the phone away and hangs up. "How old are you?"

"Thirty-six," I tell her, cancelling ten bad years.

"Thirty-six? You ought to be ashamed of yourself."

"For what, for godsake?"

But she's gone, she's out of my bedroom. My ears are

stirred. I hear her in the next room, the guest room. Throwing pillows on the floor. Pulling blankets off the bed. Opening windows, undressing–through the wall I can hear every movement she makes.

I get up and race into my guest room, repeating, "Ashamed of myself . . . what for?"

The bed in the guest room is empty.

Every light is on. I look around the room–and I see my ex-wife Sondra, naked, perched on a bookshelf.

The mole in her left cheek! I recognize it! That puffy mole with the gray hairs sticking out–or are those whiskers? A puma? She narrows her eyes and opens wet jaws. She bounds from the shelf and soars through the room, she rips my throat, she snaps my neck.

"Mom?"

Bloodied and dismembered, I see her wrinkled fingers clawing my antique gold telephone. She dials and I hear her saying, "Mom?"

Pain

Near the Boulevard Saint Germain I went flitting along sidestreets, looking for a bakery. It took me a while but sure enough I found one. A small bakery. I opened the tinkling door.

Looked very bare inside. No bread. Sold out? Nobody in the store. Or at least no one behind the counter. I knew the word for bread. *"Pain!"* I cawed toward the curtain at the back of the shop.

The curtain parted. Out came the baker—a woman in apron and glasses, squat and muscular. She had flour on her tattooed muscles. She had flour on her rimless glasses. Through whitened lenses she stared at me. *"Vous desirez?"*

"Pain," I neighed.

"Plus," said the baker lady.

Plus?

More, I supposed she meant. But I didn't need more than one loaf. So I put up one finger. *"Pain,"* I croaked.

"Plus," she insisted, turning her volume up.

Give in, I advised myself. Go ahead, buy two, how much

can bread cost? I knew how to count from one to three. So I put up two fingers and asked for two loaves. *"Deux."*

"Plus!" she exploded, her floury pink forehead turning red. *"Plus de pain!"*

I understood how vexed she must be at having to deal with a foreigner. So I yielded.

"Trois." I held up three fingers. *"Trois."*

"Plus!" she raged, and she picked up a breadknife and rushed out at me from behind the counter, waving her knife overhead with such ecstasy that her glasses fell off and hit the floor. *"Plus! Plus! Plus!"*

I got out of there as fast as I could.

In the park behind Notre Dame I sat on a bench, breathing hard.

I rummaged in my coat. Found two apricots and a packet of cheese I'd saved from lunch the day before. In my pants I found my pocketknife and cut off a wedge of cheese. Pigeons, cooing, were waddling toward my bench.

From beneath it a cat pounced, the pigeons flew up. The cat, dragging a pigeon by the throat, disappeared underneath my bench. We had lunch.

The Cat in the Colosseum

As Robin looked down between her hurrying feet, the pavement of the Via dei Fori Imperiali glared up sharply at her and hurt her eyes. She tightened her squint. She drew Gerald closer to her and increased her pace, noting again with a twinge the sound of footsteps hastening after them. They had not been in Italy long and she was still nervous at the prospect of having to speak Italian. But there was nothing she could do about it now. The driver was coming back. She would be forced to speak again. Walking quickly, she closed her eyes for just a moment. Then she heard the driver's voice behind them and knew he had caught up. *"Signore! S'accommodi!"* he called. *"Famo quattro mila lire."* He had addressed himself to Gerald, but it was Robin who would have to answer. Before she could frame in her head some reply in Italian, the driver continued, *"Non é caro, signo'! Costa poco."*

They went on walking, the driver trailing behind. Beside her Gerald turned his head from side to side. He had a large head, somewhat balding in the center, with sunken eyes and prominent lips. His lips were now rigid. Looking at him, Robin could tell by the way he turned his head and by a certain tension in his cheeks that he was trying to ignore the driver's appeals, that he wanted at all costs not to be bothered. Knowing too the fitful outbreaks of rage to which he was given, she was apprehensive. She wished she had been more firm with the Italian from the start. Suddenly the driver came up still closer behind them and began to recite in tolerable English: "We visit the Colosseum, the Catacombs of St. Calixtus, the Baths of Caracalla, the Gardens of——"

Robin interrupted. "No." Relieved at being able to speak English, she added, "I think not."

She drew her husband by the arm, turned with him into a side lane and sat down on a stone bench that seemed partially shaded, or at least mottled, by one of the young trees that lined the walks. As she sat she glanced behind her and saw the driver retreat somewhat reluctantly to his black cab, watched him grab the reins of his two horses and thought she saw his head bob jerkily up and down in a rhythm of complaint.

With a sense of discomfort she wondered—as she continually wondered—whether it was embarrassment about Gerald that created these difficulties for her. No, she thought, no, and yet it was always much less awkward when people could observe and understand without requiring explanation. And of course the driver hadn't noticed. She knew by experience that it was difficult to tell at first glance. Gerald's deep eyes were always wide open, he seemed to regard his surroundings intently.

"How far are we from the Colosseum?" he asked.

Robin shaded her eyes from the early afternoon sun and blinked at the irregular curve of stones that loomed at the other end of the avenue. "A block or so," she said. "Not much."

"Come on." He got up suddenly, dragging her with him. "Let's go."

"But we were just there yesterday."

"I want to see it again."

"And the Sistine Chapel? We don't have much time before the train leaves." (How glad she would be to leave Rome.) "What about the Sistine Chapel?"

"We'll see that too," he insisted. "Come on," he urged her along.

She turned his feet into the walk. The glare hurt, as if a rubber band had been snapped just behind the eyeballs. They hurried on, turning from the walk into the street. Almost instantly she sensed that the driver had begun to dog their steps again. His voice called out. *"Carrozza, signore?"* he shouted, still addressing Gerald. *"Solo quattro mila lire! Vedremo tutta Roma prima di sera. Annamo!"*

The muscles around Gerald's eyes grew hard. "Tell him to go away!" He spoke very loudly.

"Famo tre mila lire," the Italian called, coming up alongside them. From somewhere in the folds of his loose black coat he produced a large silver pocket watch, which he consulted. *"Se famo presto, famo a tempo. Però bisogna sbrigasse. Je facco un Prezzo bon. Du' mila lire, signo', du' mila, l'ultimo prezzo. Annamo!"* He put back the pocket watch.

"What's he saying?" Gerald demanded.

"Something about time," she whispered. "I think he wants us to hurry up and make up our minds because it's getting late. He says he'll take us for two thousand lire."

"But we've already made up our minds!" Gerald sputtered. "Give him some money. Get him away!"

Before she could think of what to say the driver had begun to speak again. Instantly Gerald sprang violently toward him. Robin almost shrieked. But she clamped one bent wrist against her teeth and forced herself to make no sound. Afraid that Gerald would fall, she was relieved to see his hands from their way unerringly, one to the Italian's shoulder, another to his shirt front. "Get away!" he yelled. "Get out of here!"

She knew now what would happen and was not afraid. She had been afraid only that he would fall. The Italian, his face contorted so that all his gold-filled teeth shone under his twisted, wide-open lips, raised one hand as though to strike and, looking up into Gerald's face, stopped. His hand came slowly down; he glanced swiftly at Robin and wrenched himself free of Gerald's hands. He staggered a few steps backward.

Robin now came up to Gerald's side. Tense but under control, she took his arm and together they crossed the Via dei Fori Imperiali. She knew it would be necessary to say nothing about his attack on the driver, knew that Gerald himself would say nothing. Out of the corner of her eye she could see the Italian still standing there where they had left him, still staring wide-eyed after them, his head pulled way down between his shoulders.

Once they had crossed the road Robin relaxed a little. She drew closer to Gerald and was comforted by his disciplined, unhesitating stride. She was taller than he, almost a head taller. Today, moreover, the effect was more than usually pronounced, for Gerald was bareheaded and she wore a blue hat that added several inches to her height. Her headed bobbed above his. She had a long, frail face with a thin white skin that seemed blue in spots, especially under the eyes and around the mouth, where tiny veins came close to the surface. Her hair too was on the pale side, a wispy shade of brown like winter grass. Against these pastel colors her eyes showed up dark and sharp, flicking about eagerly in a distracted stir. Her body, like her face, was long, with narrow hips and lean legs. Both she and Gerald wore dark blue suits, but hers was a tight fit accenting her slimness and restricting the ease of her walk. Despite the skirt her gait had a loose, boyish look to it, more lanky and more top-heavy by contrast with the balanced dignity with which her husband moved. Gerald was stocky and small; his weight, wherever he stood, appeared to have fallen solidly and intentionally onto that particular spot of ground; seemed, as it were, to have come to grips with it; when he walked in a decisive line, guided, one might imagine, by his motionless, open eyes and the turnings to and fro of his square, outsize head, which rolled like the swinging lamp of a lighthouse.

"There's a high brick wall running along the sidewalk," she said to him, wondering if he was listening, "and it's got marble tablets in it every few feet." The job of description had begun again. She glanced at the first one quickly as they passed. "They're maps of Europe showing the expansion of ancient Rome from a small city to a large empire. Each one is dated–" and she went on and on, describing the plaques in detail, reading the inscriptions and exclaiming at the extent of the Roman conquest. But she could tell from his face, from certain fine little creases and contractions around the eyes, from the hard, raised curve of his lips that he was not satisfied with her words. A familiar pain suddenly returned to clutch at her own eyes—not tears but a dryness that hurt. It had gone wrong again, she knew—but what exactly had gone wrong she asked herself? What did he want? Unhappily she tried to describe more fully, more eloquently. But eloquence was not her strong point and perhaps it was not eloquence he really wanted. She drew very close to him as they walked, desperately hoping to convey something by physical closeness alone. Though she continued to speak she grew gradually stiff—it showed even in her walk—as though many doors were closing inside her, one by one.

She understood his bitter desire to see as much of the world as he could but there were times when her part became very difficult to bear. Memorials like these, testifying to the glory of Italy, were extremely distasteful to her. Rome, she had found, was full of them; it was impossible to avoid them or the distressing memories they awoke in her. Walking the streets of the Eternal City, she felt like an exasperated worshiper before a malevolent god whom she no longer venerated, forced to pay homage, not out of fear, yet fearing to break with form and decorum. She wondered how Gerald, victim and sacrifice to the will of the god, felt beneath his alien silence. She scanned his face for an answer. His lips hung broad and joyless under the taut muscles of his cheeks. As they approached the squat, stony girth of the Colosseum she tried again to fight off the unwanted memory of an imagined battle. The fantasy was not new. In Italy, indeed, it had forced itself upon her frequently, for it had been in Italy, in the squall and flame of a small village combat during the war, that Gerald had been hit. The doctors had said he would recover but the darkness had never gone away. No one understood exactly why, neither the specialists nor, certainly, Robin herself. But much about Gerald had remained a mystery to her. When she married him he had already retreated into that dark region where she could never hope to follow.

They entered not the irregular shadow of the great stones and the afternoon sunlight seemed to gutter and go out. After an instant she could make out the way along the corridor that led, by twists, to the arena. They emerged in a few moments into the heavy glare of the amphitheater. She sat Gerald down on one of the stone benches and looked up and out to the farthest, highest edge of the broken circle. "It certainly makes you feel small," she said.

"No. No it doesn't." Gerald spoke softly and decisively, his heavy head bending toward the arena. "It makes me feel bigger than I am. These stones," he said, running his wide fingers along the broken edge of the seat, "and all this space, it's impressive, isn't it?" His broad, flat fingernails whitened along their edges as he pressed hard against the stone, testing its solidity. A tiny piece chipped off. The sharp corners of his mouth relaxed a little then and he turned his head slightly up in the sun. His face was square in outline but a little puffy in its individual features, blocked out, as it were, into distinct patches of rounded, clean-shaven skin. As he turned now, these patches and the pink balding spot over his forehead seemed sensitively tuned to the world, seemed to work separately like so many eyes, each greedily drinking in the vista of the Colosseum through the skin.

Affectionately, but aware that she had been reproved again, Robin looked at the features of his uplifted face, against which the sunlight vainly glanced. He seemed to be sealed in. And yet, she thought, the darkness in which he lived was not a wall without a chink but a void, an absence, a blank where light knocked but no tenant rose to answer. In that void and despite it, she knew, Gerald seemed always to appreciate and to enjoy whatever they visited more fully than she whose eyes were free to see. It occurred to her that vision might at times be an impediment. She found it difficult to accept the thought. Perhaps Gerald, absorbing the promise and not the reality, saw the unseen on faith, conjured up a vision in which the will to see made him happier than the sight itself. Perhaps . . . and yet his face now, as she examined it, positively glowed with an appreciation that seemed real enough. It was certainly more than she could muster up, anxious as she was about her husband's enjoyment and lost in a fog of questions. For something about his appreciation bothered her, had bothered her indeed for a long time–sometimes to the point of acute pain. She sensed that it was too scrupulous an enjoyment. Unable to believe fully in its sincerity, she had strong but ill-defined feelings of discomfort. Uneasy now in the renewed presence of her suspicion, she tried to clear her thoughts. She looked down past Gerald to the arena floor, where crumbling masonry still outlined what had once been a maze of subterranean rooms and corridors; she thought of the martyred souls who had gone trustingly to a Lord they could not see.

Gerald spoke. "I'd like to get up a little higher."

Robin took his hand and together they climbed over the stone seats. But the seats were high and Gerald seemed ill at ease. Finally they came to the end of the first bank of rows and had to make their way along a wall to a passageway that led them under the seats and up again to the next tier. But here the going became still more difficult. Rubble, scattered everywhere on the seats, got under Gerald's feet; each of his steps had to be guided. Several times he slipped on the crumbling stone and Robin had to catch him, anxious lest he fall among those high rows. Finally, when they had struggled almost halfway up the second tier, they recognized that it was impossible to keep going, and Gerald said: "I think I'll rest here. You go on."

She left him then, glad to be alone, and climbed by herself, her long legs working hard. When she came to the end of the second tier she found another passageway and followed it under and up to the third tier. When she got to the top of that she stopped. Curious to observe her husband now that he too was alone, yet oddly apprehensive of what she might find, she looked swiftly down at Gerald, tiny and dark against the vast expanse of white stone. He was bent over, sitting down. For a moment the thought occurred to her that he might be in the throes of a sudden cramp but she quickly told herself not to let her imagination run off with her. Gerald, she knew, was probably tying his shoelaces or perhaps running his fingers along the stone floor and seat. Still thinking of him, fondly and uncomfortable at once, and still breathing quickly, she looked out above the opposite wall of the Colosseum where the sky hung spotless, the color of clean but faded blue wallpaper. The world seemed to rest for a moment in silence. It was one of those clear, windless times when one can see far, though there was nothing to see but sky, when one seems to expand peacefully into the distance and to feel that one can, after all, get to the bottom of things. Robin thought of Gerald, tried to fathom his existence. Somewhere beneath his gestures and moods and willful reactions that she knew so thoroughly lay an undiscovered country; of that she was certain. His blindness functioned for her as an intricate, protective mask beyond which she could not go. And in a sense she too acted as his protection against the world. He was almost in every way dependent on her, leaving it to her from the start to handle all the arrangements one had to make for living and traveling, all the unforeseeable situations and encounters that arose while sight-seeing, virtually everything except decisions about where to go and what to see. Yet when, after all these outside encounters, she turned to him as any wife must turn to any husband, she found that some interior chain held him away from her—shy, perhaps, or secretive.

She had known, of course, when she married him the kind of life she would have. But the knowledge had not frightened her. She had looked forward with unmistakable joy to the prospect of her new dedication. The earlier love with which she had first promised, when he had still been whole, to marry him had been not nearly so strong or so tender as the love with which, finally, she had become his wife. No physical accident, she knew, could alter the fact of their love or break the promise she had freely given him before that accident. Afterward she had given him that promise as freely again. And silently now, secretly, she repeated it to herself at times when her anguish become too piercing to bear. She wanted desperately to be Gerald's fulfillment. But always aware of her inadequacies, she suffered without speaking, from moment to moment, as she knew Gerald too suffered and said nothing.

In Italy the tension between them had grown worse. For in

remembrance, she thought, of that ultimate moment when the burst of an Italian shell had torn the light from him, his heart had grown quietly cold with unpersuadable anger. He had come to care for only one thing, and to care for it violently. He seemed to feel that to see Italy was to conquer it, as though by forcing himself–foreigner and enemy–into all its holiest places and most ancient monuments he could triumph over it and retrieve the full measure of his dignity. She was sure that some such element of gloating stained his fervor for Italy. In any case he brooked no interference with the sustained, tireless and almost fanatic ardor with which he searched out and fed upon its treasures. Always liable to outburst of taut violence, his temper now was strained and, worst of all, his reason seemed on a perilous edge. He wreaked his pain and pride on everyone, on Italians, on his own countrymen, even on Robin herself, until she was sometimes ready to cry out and run, to leave the details, the arrangements, the talking and planning to him, blind as he was, lest she who once had loved should grow to hate. But always at the last extremity she halted, transfixed by a question. What and who was he? She dismissed, on faith, the obvious, would not accept the surface of identity that customarily seals a man away from too close an investigation. At desperate moments she would search in fury for the missing testimony.

She looked down again along the tiers of white stone rows and started: Gerald was nowhere in sight. She scanned the amphitheater for a trace of him. Every inch of the white expanse was open to view. Was it possible he had left the Colosseum? But he could never have made his way to the corridor, she thought. She hesitated, bewildered, thinking that there must be some obstruction, some stanchion, post or corner behind which he might temporarily be hidden. But there was none. Every seat and every stone was clearly visible in the sharp sunlight. Unable to believe, she checked again no possible protection. There could be no doubt about it. He was gone.

She did not give herself time to think; she descended as quickly as she could to where she had left him. But the going was difficult and often precarious. She found it necessary to watch her footing carefully because of the rubble. Her tight skirt and high heels made matters still worse. She had to jump down between the high rows, covered all the way with rocks and broken bits of masonry. When she finally emerged from the passageway she saw Gerald sitting again, exactly as she had left him, in the very same spot. She made her way more slowly now, but still with some difficulty, down to his side. When at last she had almost reached his level she saw that he had in his lap a small, bedraggled cat. The cat, its yellow markings undulating sensitively along its back, was receiving Gerald's attentions somewhat dubiously. As Gerald stroked and petted it, the cat hissed. And with that insufficient warning it bit Gerald's finger and leaped from his lap to the row below. Gerald swung at it furiously and hit it in midair, catching it along its hindquarters and sending it spinning against the stone. But the cat hardly seemed to hit the stone, or rather it rebounded sideways with such surprising energy that its motion seemed to avoid the stone and land it in a single swoop three rows below. It crouched there, bent completely around like a crescent, eyes round and ears back, tensely challenging pursuit and backing away.

Startled by Gerald's uncanny aim, Robin climbed down over the last row and sat down at his side. He stood up immediately. Whether he had been surprised by her arrival at just that moment she could not tell. He said: "Let's get out of here!" His face had the hard, square look of visor clamped sharply down.

She took his hand. Going down was even more difficult for Gerald than going up. The jumps were rather hard to calculate and Robin found herself unable to give really adequate guidance. But she held on gently, and in any case Gerald did not fall.

The cat, keeping its attention circumspectly on them, preceded them by deft leaps to the passageway. It disappeared cautiously inside. And indeed, once they were in the passage Robin wished for the eyes of a cat as she stumbled about (she knew how jarring this was to Gerald) searching for the proper turn to the exit. As her eyes adjusted to the reduced light she tried to fathom Gerald's disappearance. The only place he might have been when she had looked and found him missing was inside one of the passages. Perhaps he had gone in search of the cat–had heard it and followed it and brought it back with him. And yet, she reasoned, it was utterly unthinkable that he could have made his way back and forth to one of the passageways, all that distance up or down among the littered seats and then back again. Even if it were possible, why should he want to? It was much too precarious an undertaking; indeed, quite impossible, she was convinced. Yet without a doubt he had been out of sight when she had looked. Unless– unless for some reason he had actually been there, in his seat in plain sight, and she had been unable to see him–but how absurd! She was not blind. Yet how had he walked?

All at once they emerged into the sun. Robin blinked. She looked at Gerald but his face was tense and she did not want to speak. The muscles in his cheeks were throbbing and on the spot where he was getting bald she could see traces of thin moisture under the fine, meager hairs. She shrank from pressing for an answer, not sure of what an answer might mean or where it might take her, not willing to find out.

They went by taxi to the Vatican and got out at an entrance to the museum. Their dark suits, as they mounted the wide stone stairs that led to the entrance, stood out sharply against the discolored but glittering stone. Gerald marched steadily and firmly up. But the stairs were widely spaced and Robin's skirt pulled taut against her knees at each step. Inside the lobby, ornate with gilt pillars and elaborate moldings, stood a number of men, some uniformed, some in light topcoats, some in work clothes, all seeming rather restless. They stared at the visitors as they came in. Robin felt slightly confused. She went to the ticket window. "We would like to see the Sistine Chapel," she said.

"*E troppo tardi,*" replied the man behind the window, folding his glasses and putting them away.

Too late? she thought. But it can't be too late. She looked at her watch. It was not quite half-past three. She spoke to the man again, still in English. "What time do you close?"

"*E troppo tardi,*" he repeated, either not understanding or not caring. He was busy closing boxes and straightening up. The others in the lobby looked on dispassionately.

Robin returned apprehensively to her husband, who had

remained standing in a little alcove some distance away. She felt a great pressure in her head and a disconcerting flutter in her arms and stomach, knowing how he would react to her words. "He says it's too late," she told him.

"The hell it is!" Gerald insisted. "Tell him we want to see the Sistine Chapel." His voice was becoming loud. Robin recognized the tone.

As she moved toward the ticket window she felt as if she were being sent as a sacrifice into a ritual she did not understand. She moved clumsily, trying to think of the right words in Italian. Her heels clicked loudly over the marble floor. Her hands hung down inertly but gingerly, as though on springs, brushing against her skirt as she walked. With her large eyes open to the full she looked about her, searching for some flaw in the ceremony on which to base a fantastic, last-minute refusal to participate. At the window she saw a sign, two lines in Italian that she understood: the chapel closed at a quarter to four but the sale of tickets to the chapel ended at half-past three. She glanced at her watch, which read three-twenty-nine, and still pointing to the dial she showed the watch to the man at the window. "It's not three-thirty yet," she said, tapping the sign. *"Non è ora."*

The Italian distractedly shoved his own watch across the wooden counter, indicating the time with his other hand, and Robin was surprised to find their watches agreed. "There!" she cried. "I told you!" She tapped her watch excitedly. "You see we still have time! *Abbiamo tempo!*"

The Italian regarded his own watch unmoved. He shrugged his shoulders He moved away, taking his coat off a hook and muttering something in Italian. But it was too swift and Robin missed it. Finally he returned. *"Mi dispiace,"* he whispered. Robin remained totally confused. He repeated: *"E troppo tardi, signora."*

She returned to Gerald quickly. "They won't let us in. I tried. We're too late." She was miserable, for herself and Gerald both.

Gerald's face grew white. His lower lip began to twitch as though in pain. He stepped out into the hall and turned his head toward a group of men. He spoke in a strident baritone. "We want to see the Sistine Chapel. Will someone please show us the way to the Sistine Chapel!" His feet were planted far apart and firmly on the ground, and one shoulder was turned out at an angle as though he were expecting a blow. "What's the matter?" he called out. "Doesn't anybody here understand English?" The words rang against the high ceiling.

Robin went to his side. "Never mind," she whispered. "They don't understand anyway."

Gerald seemed not to notice her. "Sis-tine Chapel!" he sang out, enunciating the syllables. "Sis-tine Chapel! Michelangelo! Sis-tine Chapel! Understand? We want to see the Chapel."

He walked a few paces farther into the room, turning his body and face in a new direction. The bystanders stared at him without comprehension. One of them whispered quickly.

"What's that?" Gerald shouted. What'd you say?"

Robin came up again and took his arm. He shook her away, carefully but angrily. "Tell them we're leaving Rome tonight." he shouted. "Tell them we've got to see the Sistine Chapel today. We're leaving tonight. Tell them I said I've seen everything there is to see in the goddam town and it all stinks and the one damn thing I really want to see is the Sistine Chapel and I'm going to see it!"

Through the door by which they had entered, a special guard now came in. His uniform, a gorgeous array of blues and reds trimmed with gold, glittered as he crossed a patch of sunlight, his cape trailing behind in an arc, his huge hat sitting perfectly upright on his unsmiling face. He began to talk to the nearest spectator.

The sound of voices conversing at normal pitch not very far from him produced a remarkable change in Gerald. He spun around quickly in the direction of the voices as though discovering all at once among his hearers an instance of defiance or of indifference. Unexpectedly, he threw up his hands as though to ward off a blow to the head. At the same time his face, white but immobile, began suddenly to twitch and tremble, his unblinking eyes to palpitate with the rest of his face. Then slowly but firmly he began to yell, almost to cry out, in a higher pitch than any he had used before: *"Ascoltate, bastardi! Sono Americano, capite? Uno di voi bastardi m'ha colpito agli ochi in Guerra, ma io vi dico che andrò vedere la Cappella Sistina!"*

Robin, standing by herself in the center of the lobby, felt the world all around began to escape from her at terrific speed, like the rush of an uncontrollable wind. With a plunging sensation she blacked out, putting out her hand at the last instant of consciousness to save herself from falling on the floor. But she did not fall and the blackness vanished swiftly. A few of his words had reached her, vibrant even in the blackness: *. . . you bastards. . . my eyes in the war ... I tell you I'm going to see the Chapel. . .* Understanding only so much, she was left standing, paralytically confused at the flow of Italian, which she knew to be impossible, from her husband's lips. *"Ascoltate. Idioti, dite un prezzo. Abbiamo il denaro, capite? Quanto costa per entrare qui?"* His voice still rang out stridently, and the phrases, a few of them, came to her with stinging ease: *. . . idiots! . . . we've got money . . . how much does it cost? . . .* The words, so strange-sounding in her own ears, had an extraordinary resonance even among the pillars of the marble lobby, where everything save his wild monologue was now hushed. *"La Cappella Sistina! Michelangelo! Voglio vederla! Quanto volete?"*

The guard, who with all the other spectators had been eyeing Gerald for several moments, now approached soberly and addressed himself to Gerald.

"Signore, se desidera vedere la Cappella—"

"Va ben. Quanto volete?"

"Ma no! Niente. Ma la Cappella chiuderà fra dieci minuti, e devono correre, ma presto, presto!" He waved his hands urgently, the gold brocade on his sleeves describing several bright little arcs.

"Va bene," Gerald said, and turned toward Robin. "He says we'll have to run if we want to make it."

Robin found herself utterly unable to speak. Gerald, standing several feet from her, dwarfed by the height of the tall guard in his still taller, outlandish hat, looked smaller than she remembered him to be and in a way foreign too. But she went to him and took his hand, helpless before the discovery of an unaccountable secret and unable to think about it.

They began to trot down the corridor. Gerald murmured

something to her. "He said they're going to close the place in ten minutes. Come on. We're going to run."

There were signs all along the way indicating the direction of the chapel. Robin held on tightly to Gerald's arm, dazed and uncomprehending but able mechanically to act as her husband's guide. They raced along the thin strip of carpeting that ran in a straight line from room to room and corridor to corridor. Along the walls and windows at each side a row of heads, busts and small statues, each on its pedestal, fled behind them as they ran. Robin's long legs flung her lanky body forward, graceless beside her husband's even padding gait. Suddenly she slipped, her ankle twisted and hurt. She stopped and said, "Just a second, Gerald." My heels are too high." She took off her shoes quickly and they began to run again, past all the exhibits in the museum, along each wing of the building. Huge paintings in darkened rooms glared down at them. Several times Robin thought she would have to stop but Gerald's dogged pace kept her moving, on and on. She sensed that she was being led, that she had gradually become the follower and Gerald the leader. When at last they reached the chapel, it was practically empty. Several people seemed about to leave, and in the corner an old man in a black suit, evidently a guard, was looking at his watch. Robin paused a moment in the center of the chapel, trying to catch her breath. She held Gerald's hand in her own grimly. Then she looked up. Over the altar and spreading out to all corners of the walls and ceiling an immense vista of frescoes seemed to light the room with a subdued inner blue radiance of their own. She looked straight up over her head and saw God and the creation of Adam, a vision that looked like an arrested wave. It was several moments before she could take her eyes away from it. By then, much moved and quieted, she sat Gerald down on one of the benches and tried to breathe regularly. "The ceilings and the walls," she whispered, "are all covered with pictures." She began to describe them but her mind ached with the weight of many questions she could not bring herself to ask. Instead she tried to speak and think normally. She tried to decide whether to tell him which biblical scenes were portrayed or to explain how they were arranged in the chapel or to try to express the details of the color and design. Before she had well begun, however, a look on his face stopped her. Something pained and independent had manifested itself in the unusual slight lowering of his eyelids and the turn of his neck and cheek away from her. She stopped speaking and drew breaths. With the gradual return of natural breathing, the realization slowly awoke in her that it would indeed be senseless to continue her pretense. Her trust in her role was gone. She could no longer consider herself Gerald's guide. Some part of her stepped back hurriedly from the thought with positive fright.

She wandered off by herself then, leaving Gerald sitting alone against the wall. She looked up again at the ceiling and saw, this time, the creation of Eve. It was not as pleasing to her as the creation of Adam; it was, she felt, quite inferior, and she was disappointed. She turned away, glancing at the frescoes over the altar. People were beginning to leave. The guard was looking at his watch again. She found it difficult to concentrate. She turned her attention with effort to the story of Noah and his drunkenness, to the scene of David killing Goliath.

But how—she asked herself at last, oblivious of what she

saw, and forcing the question into expression—and where and when had he learned Italian? The answer came at the same instant, as though implied in the question. In Italy, of course, during the war. Yet never spoken? Never mentioned? She drew in her breath softly. She felt as though she were in the presence of a sacred mystery about to be revealed, and the sensation was not comfortable. She turned to look at Gerald. He was still seated at the rear of the chapel, his head thrown back, gazing interminably at the ceiling.

Her left hand caught at her long thigh as though to quiet her. Why had he gagged his Italian? She searched for a clear decision. Out of hate or, perhaps, fear, she thought. Had he then denied the language or had he quite, in fact, forgotten it, sunk it deep within the uncontrollable wells of memory? Her own memory pained her now almost to the point of frenzy as she recalled all those never-ending, needless moments when she had been forced to speak the foreign tongue. Perhaps his deceit had been out of reach, his reach as well as hers. The depth of his dependence worried her; she wondered what extent of fury lay concealed beneath it.

She clutched her shoes more tightly in her right hand so that the fingers hurt, aware now for the first time that she was carrying them. She gazed down at her stockinged feet. Her left foot had begun to swell. She felt old, sore and lame.

She looked up then, her attention fixed once again by the figure of Eve rising out of Adam's side. Something about this portrait insulted her, some absence of intelligence in Eve with which she might have faced that primal moment, the look perhaps of a beast or idiot born without advance notice to human maturity, a kind of winsome stupidity. And Adam, his eyes closed, lay sleeping in a smug peace. She sensed a sinister intention in all this, whether on the part of God or the painter.

She glanced back at Gerald, struck all at once by a panic ray of fear. He sat against the wall, his head turned up at a comfortable angle, staring without shame at the frescoes. His face was alight with the gentle look of one whose inmost wants have at last been satisfied. The sweetness of his look pained her, the confession of his peace stabbed at her. She watched with involuntary doubt. Trapped more tightly every instant by an unwanted horror, she watched Gerald's eyes, the clear pupils shifting now and then amid the unblemished white. The angle of his tilted head communing with the ancient frescoes overhead chilled her with the remembrance of the cat in the Colosseum, of his impossible disappearance, of his unerring attack on the driver, of the birth of the Italian language on his tongue, and of a hundred lost, extravagant imaginings. All at once she understood. She had the sense, no longer imminent but fulfilled, of a pure revelation. At this extremity her body, in a natural and will-less reflex, shuddered fitfully. Gerald continued to sit before her eyes, callous and immovable, a haunting vision obedient only to the blinding rhythm of her fury. She watched his lips, his eyes. She could not possibly be mistaken.

She made a strong, single attempt to bring down the mask again, to retreat to the world of warm and proper sacrifice. She put a hand out toward Gerald but her feet would not move. She saw him begin to get up now. At the same moment, at the corner of her vision, she saw the guard. He was standing at the door, holding it open, watch in hand, waiting.

From Hand to Mouth

The drive from my mother's house to my father's apartment took an hour. He had left my mother while she was pregnant with my sister, and when my mother went to the maternity hospital I slept on his couch for almost a week. Mealtimes impressed me. A *man* kept feeding me. I couldn't account for it. He gave me breakfast, lunch, and dinner. He dipped a spoon into a bowl and raised a spoonful of soup to his moustache, blew on it, blew on it again, then tilted it to my mouth and burned my lips.

He had a basement apartment. Several gloomy rooms all in a row–and the gloomiest was the one I slept in. to cheer things up he had hung a gaudy tapestry over my couch. It mesmerized me by day. At night I could still see it hanging over me.

A swordsman held a child by one ankle. He held the child up at arm's length, in mid-air, with its head twisting downward. High above the child he held his sword, ready to slice. A woman jeered. Another woman begged. A king or a judge watched calmly. Solomon–but I didn't know that then.

What I saw was a boy in trouble, a naked boy who had no say in the matter.

I can fix with certainty the day of the year I became the swordsman. July Fourth, it must have been–because my mother was planning to take my sister and me to a parade that afternoon. In our back yard, that's where I was sitting, waiting in the heat. All dressed up in a sailor suit. My sister, wearing a puffy pink dress over her diaper, looked so pretty that I noticed her. She was wavering toward me through the grass.

I can see the next few minutes with undiminished clarity. I see the broken-stemmed dandelions bowing to the grass, I see my sister's knees collapsing. Though I'm wearing short pants I can't see my own knees: there's a glare in the way. The whiteness of a drawing pad glares from my lap. A spot of purple. It's not on the page. There's a crayon in my hand, poised.

The chair I had been told to sit in was a folding chair. Beside it stood a second chair, unoccupied. Both chairs had metal legs of rusted chrome. They had canvas seats. Striped canvas, blue and green. With plastic armrests, mottled green. Since the two chairs stood side by side, their armrests were touching–or so one might have thought.

My sister had fallen. She fell on all fours, undismayed. She picked herself up and stood still, swaying a little before she tottered on. Both her arms were outstretched with determination to reach the empty chair next to mine. Her face was a balloon, her cheeks were inflated with joy, and it was this happiness that held her up. She wobbled. She was almost there. She fell again. She hesitated, tried to get up, but she was so close now, it hardly mattered. On her knees she entered the shade cast by the seat of the unoccupied chair, disappearing from my sight.

Although my mother was invisible to me all this while, she commanded a perfect view of our back yard from where she stood indoors. She was washing up the breakfast dishes while she watched through the screened-in window at the rear of the house.

So far I had drawn nothing. I looked down at the tempting blankness. I put the tip of my crayon to the pad. Out of nowhere an ant appeared. A live ant, motionless, stunned for an instant, had fallen on my page as though I had drawn it. It crawled.

My startled crayon jerked after it, following its progress. Here, there, squiggles of purple. Never before had I drawn anything so interesting. I nudged it, I pushed it, I had only to touch that ant, and it fled, it raced, leading me on—each time in a new direction. It eluded me; I concentrated. It veered, I gave chase. I outflanked it, blocking it, keeping it from reaching the edge of my page, careful not to hurt it.

At last I was satisfied. I let it go because I liked my picture just as it was. In my eyes I had produced a marvel, the portrait of an ant. I lost myself in the contemplation of my purple maze.

The ant reappeared on the green plastic armrest of my chair, where it ran, hesitated, still excited, reaching out repeatedly for the armrest of the chair my sister was under—waving its antennae as if not convinced it could cross, sensing a crevasse, a separation too fine for me to see.

A shove from my crayon swept it across the gap.

In a hurry to follow its progress, I got up. I dropped my pad, dropped my crayon, forgot my drawing. The ant, scurrying purposefully earthward, had traveled down the metal supports of the armrest until it reached the edge of the striped canvas seat. Another hesitation there. A wavering, a quivering of feelers in air. An interrogation of its head, rotating. A decision with its forelegs: it began to traverse the canvas seat. I turned to sit down. I did more than sit down. I threw myself backward onto the seat of the chair in order to crush my ant.

My sister screamed.

It cannot be said that she grew up mutilated. By the time she reached her teens, for example, she had mastered the violin, and from then on she was able to give my mother and me nightly pleasure with tones that were unwaveringly pure. To the best of my knowledge her psyche bore no scar; and she held no grudge against me.

The chrome legs of the hair she was playing beneath had not been fully spread apart on the ground–almost but not quite. Her left pinky finger–not all of it, only the very tip–had curled its way into one of the metal hinges. When I thumped down on the seat, the metal legs spread open, the metal hinge snapped shut, my sister's fingertip flew off.

At her shriek, I glanced down. I saw it. An unexpected pinkness, a surprise in the grass. Not unlike a pencil eraser. But it was perfectly clear to me what it was. With the smallest of shudders I picked it up to examine it. An ant had dropped out of the sky. And now here was another trick.

Cause and effect? An ant–no, not just an ant, *my ant*. I had captured it, surrounded it, drawn its picture, studied its habits, and squashed it. What a day. What a performance! Next a piece of my sister. Boneless apparently. Almost bloodless. Spongy. A fraction of the first joint of an exceedingly small finger. My first impulse was to pocket this prize. I had earned it. My second impulse (my sister was making a great deal of noise) was to return it to her in order to quiet her down.

But already my mother had come running out of the house, and my third impulse was overpowering. Hide the evidence. I palmed it, clutching it in my fist.

Concealment didn't work. My mother, as she scooped up my wounded sister, knocked me out of the chair and called me a string of names. Obscenities, unheard-of, unrepeatable– unrepeatable because I can't recall for sure which ones she used. But I can guess. Because over the years she frequently conveyed her estimate of her only son in phrases that varied hardly at all. She maintained even afterward that it was damn lucky my baby sister hadn't put her neck into the hinge of that chair (physically impossible though that would have been) since I would surely have seized the opportunity.

"You vicious little pisser," said my mother, "murdering little bastard," or words to that effect.

"Accident," I yelled. "Ant," I shrilled. "It was an ant!"

But she never would listen. Away she dashed, with me trailing behind, shouting at the top of my lungs, pleading from the bottom of my heart, begging her to believe me.

My sister, howling louder than I could, was carried upstairs to the bathroom where first-aid supplies were kept.

I didn't dare go up, not at first. Tiny though it was, my sister's severed pinky tip had begun to feel monstrously large in my hand. *Should* I return it to her?–maybe so, but I lingered at the foot of the stairs for several minutes before I found the courage to put my foot on the first step.

I started up–wavering, I imagine, like my sister among the dandelions, like my ant at the crevasse–drawn upward by a moral sense of property, the desire to reunite the tidbit in my outstretched fist with my sister's flesh. Pulled downward and sideways by other forces. That brand-new surge of self-esteem. And something else–wonder. Expansive wonder, wonder at flesh itself, at fatality and chance, and a stubborn piggish wonder at my own astounding feat. By rights, the enormity in my hand was mine, my trophy, my reward–did I have to give it back? I mounted, step by step.

Just then my mother came barging out of the bathroom on her way downstairs to search for the doctor's phone number. Comforting my sister, she held her in one arm. She also held a pair of scissors she'd been using to cut strips of gauze bandages. The loose end of a bandage flapped behind her like a kite tail as she came flying straight at me.

She used her knee. I bumped to the bottom of the steps. The steps were carpeted and I suffered no memorable bruises. My mother caught up with me at the foot of the stairs, where she remarked in passing, "I ought to slice it off, snip, snip." Oh yes, she actually said that. But though she snapped her scissors near the short pants of my sailor suit, she sliced nothing. She kicked me. Not there. I don't recall where; in the head, I think.

She dialed for the doctor.

All this time I hadn't let go of my prize, not even as I fell. Were my eyes wet? Of course they were, but so was my mouth. I put it in there.

What did it taste like, that tender bit of my sister's meat?

Even now I have no trouble recollecting its complex flavor. It tasted to me like glory and spite, a mixture of sugar and worms, spice and snails, everything nice and puppydogs' tails.

"Once upon a time a greenheaded carrot was driving down the road with a diamond ring in the pocket of his shirt."

My sister, listening closely, ate some carrots.

"He drove and he drove until he saw a girl on a bike, a little girl whose name was peas."

"That's not a name."

She had to follow the rules. I wouldn't go on till she had eaten some peas. I held the fork to her lips and tilted it. She opened her mouth and took a few.

I went on, "Her name was peas because she drank so much water."

"Wise guy," said my mother. She made this comment from the kitchen, where she was drying dishes. "Don't be so smart."

"Milk, okay? Peas drank only milk, she even swam in milk."

My sister managed a sip or two. "How come the carrot had a ring?"

"Because he had to find a wife. So he stopped his car and put his orange hand in his pocket and stuck his green head out of the window, and he showed off his diamond ring to the little girl. Peas, said Mr. Carrot, is your mother Mrs. Chicken married to anyone?"

Beginning to take an interest in her food, my sister nibbled at her cut-up chicken, carrots, and peas. She asked me, "*Was* she married?"

"Oh no, not her, replied little peas. *Once* she was married. But not any more."

In the kitchen a plate was dropped. It shattered.

"You!" my mother exploded. "Look what you did!"

From the time I was seven I seldom saw my father, except for one month during the summer. Once a year, to give my mother a break I suppose, he took my sister and me off her hands. We got heat rashes, sitting in the back of his car for hours while he drove us into the mountains. He always rented a bungalow at a resort in the Adirondacks, the same tiny house each July, close to a creek.

I liked my sister well enough in the city. But in the country, every night, she turned into a coward. She was afraid of the dark. And when darkness fell my father, for his convenience, would put the two of us to sleep at the same late hour, in the same big bed. Lights out, kids, he'd say. Out they would go.

And off *he* would go. To the "main house" or the nearby casino, to play bingo or pinochle.

He knew how my sister would shiver. She would begin whining before he left. But he refused to pamper her. In forbidding us to have even the smallest light on in that bungalow, no doubt he thought he could teach her to sleep the way I once saw him teach a pup to swim, by throwing her into the blackness.

Alone with her, I would insist, "What's so scary? So you're in the dark and can't see–so what?"

"What happened to the walls?" she would whimper. "Is the bathroom okay?"

I had to get out of the bed and bang on the walls. "Hear

that? Walls." I flushed the toilet. I ran the water in the sink. "Any more questions?"

"Am I pointed right?"

Every night, more questions. "Am I straight in the bed? I can't see my feet. Am I sideways, will I fall out? How far away is the floor? What happened to the walls?"

A philosophical panic, in retrospect. A pesky metaphysician, my sister was. An epistemological nag. Is there anything? Are we anywhere, and what makes you so sure? She deprived me of sleep until–exhausted–I hit upon a cure. The only convincing one.

"Here," I said, at wit's end. "Give me your hand."

I found her wrist in the blackness of the bed. I took her hand and opened it.

"Can you hold this?" I asked, pushing my left thumb into her palm. "It's my flashlight," I explained. She knew it was my thumb, of course she did. But her small fingers encircled it at once.

"If you need any light, just press the trigger," I said. The tip of my thumb protruded. She squeezed it. "Look," I said. "See? It works."

Like a charm. My opposable flashlight threw a beam into the corners of her fears more illuminating than the bulbs of reality. "Shine me on the chifforobe," I suggested. She squeezed. The shadowy chest loomed closer, intensely comforting, visible to us both. "Point me over there. Not there! At the wallpaper. See the flowers?"

"They're pink," she noticed, shining my thumb on them. "Where's the chair?–oh look!" She saw it. "There. With my shoes underneath!"

Sometimes, whether in eagerness or anxiety, she'd hurt my thumbnail. When it hurt I discovered that I could not only see the pattern of roses on the walls; I could count the number of petals on the unopened buds. When my sister dropped into sleep still clasping my thumb I also noticed that if I strained my eyes a little I could even make out the shape of the urn on the shoulder of the nymph on the calendar by the phone near the door in the next room.

That large art calendar had impressed me for the several years running. My father never took it down. Each July I'd return, somewhat more impressionable, to the same maiden on the wall: the same reproduction in color of an ideal nude. I wonder, didn't she fade a bit–year by year? I imagine not. Those summers were out of time, and the girl was immortal. Woman, I should say–for to me she appeared overpoweringly mature. And to my father? If I'm not mistaken he seems to have regarded her as a household deity. He kept her by the phone, securely nailed, and never thought of turning to any other month.

At first I thought of her only as the knock-kneed lady with the jug on one shoulder. A dimwit–or else why would she be carrying that jug around without any clothes on? The more I pondered her, the more difficult became the puzzles she teased me with. For instance, what did she have in the depths of her jug–milk? honey? hot cocoa?–what did she have at the cusp of her legs–and why if I so much as stared at her jug did the back of my throat grow parched?

That Adirondack resort my father frequented may have been designed to tantalize small boys with thirsty minds. Its two most crowded attractions were a couple of spots along the creek where bathing suits were never worn. Known as the Men's B.A. and the Women's B.A., these sites consisted of hot flat rocks and shallow pools. The initials stood for Bare Ass. Unfortunately, a bend in the creek concealed the two B.A.'s from each other. Little puzzlers like me, wading upstream in the buff, had to have gumption. If you had gumption enough to wade up along that very shallow stream to the point where they could see you, you could obtain a long-distance view of any number of nude grandmothers, aunts, possibly even a cousin or two.

The trouble was, at that distance there was simply no telling what lurked between their legs.

So I put on my swimtrunks one day and took the overland route through no-man's land. Darting from tree to tree, ducking behind boulders, crawling under bushes, wriggling on my belly and risking poison ivy, I sneaked toward knowledge like an inchworm in the grass. Closer? Nothing doing. A hundred yards from my goal, all gumption failed. I hardly dared to raise my head. When I did, what I saw looked like a herd of pale seals sunning themselves on the rocks at the zoo.

And then the herd moved. I didn't realize at first what the uproar was all about, why it was that several of my prey had begun to laugh, then the rest of them—cackling laughter—a commotion of animal flesh. Hooting at me? They had spotted me and were pointing me out to each other, applauding my efforts. But in the tranquil woods the clapping of their hands sounded like gunfire.

I hopped from under my cover and raced away, running till

I was out of breath, hoping to God I hadn't been recognized. I was still panting when I reached our bungalow.

Father never kept it locked. I pulled our screen door. It creaked that's all, and after that warning creak there was nothing to stop me. In the drawer of the chifforobe I found what I needed. Scissors. I hurried to the telephone. To the maiden with the jug on one shoulder, naked on the wall.

I took her down. I held her upside down, I snipped all around her, freeing her from yesteryear, cutting her off from eternity.

Then I carried her off to the woods. Alone with that beauty, I held her at arm's length. My scissors were raised, ready to slice. In the greenish light I looked up at the trees. They were watching me calmly. They weren't even shivering in the hot wind.

With the blades of the scissors I snipped upward along her ankles and calves. I unlocked her knees. I parted her thighs. She looked sad but not surprised. I put my mouth to her face and took the first bite.

Moving downward, I tried her neck, her shoulders, her breasts. I took bits and pieces of her midsection. I didn't swallow her. I chewed her, tasting her a little more fully with every bite. She tasted as I imagined a mature dandelion would taste—the exotic tartness of green leaves, the syrupy sourness of yellow tendrils. I took my time, eating her. I wanted to put off, as long as possible, the moment when she would be entirely known.

Slinking out of the woods at last, I kept her in a chewy wet wad lodged between my gums and my cheek. With my tongue I nudged her. Between my teeth I pressed her. I carried her around for hours, digesting my first woman.

The Anatomy of a Poet

Coarse? Well, maybe I am. One of the magazines called me a "coarse old lady poet." I won't argue the point. Naturally, I got coarser as I grew older, like most of you. I don't mean only my indecent turn of mind, which comes automatically with age; I mean those mannerisms which even lady poets develop and which never get into print: I can rarely eat without getting food all over my mouth. And these days whenever I eat anything I really enjoy, I make a sharp whining involuntary noise under my chewing – I can hardly control it. And the smell of my feet, which has gotten stronger with age like cheese – well, would it really shock you if I said I like it? I think not, at least not if you've reached my age. But just in case, I want to warn you: even if you happen to have read some of my verse and thought the sweet-and-sour of it to your taste, prose is another matter. For I think you'll agree with me that it isn't life itself which is coarse, but the way in which it's experienced. And though I've always written about my life in poetry, I experienced it, so to speak, in prose – physically and corruptly.

For example, the first time I wrote a poem I was very

troubled by the problem of rhyme (I was eight years old) and I was scratching my behind all during the composition. I remember it distinctly because my Uncle Lemmie (dead a long while now. The only thing I remember about him is that he was always pushing a garden wheelbarrow. When other children talked about their fathers' Fords, I used to brag that my Uncle Lemmie pushed me around in a wheelbarrow) saw me scratching and told me that little ladies didn't, not anywhere. He lowered the handles of the wheelbarrow gravely as he said it, sat down on the bench beside me, and began tenderly braiding my hair. "What're you doing, Millie?" he said.

"Writing a poem. What rhymes with fire?"

"Lots of things. Tire, or fire . . ."

"I've already got fire."

"Well, then spire."

We were sitting across the street from my house. Inside through the porch windows I could see my father reading the Sunday paper, and my mother playing the piano, and over by the cellar door the smoke which seemed to be coming from the garden where my uncle had been gathering dead leaves and burning them. I had a school copybook on my lap and a pencil in the hand that wasn't scratching. My knees, sticking out beyond the hem of my skirt, were dirty as usual, this time with coal dust, and I moved the copybook cautiously along my skirt with the tip of the pencil while my uncle was busy with my hair, to cover my knees. He said, "How come you're writing poetry?"

"Because I've got something extra important to say to Mommy and Daddy. And I can't use spire."

"Well, let me see what you got so far."

I want to tell you right away
About a big red fire,
That if you want the house to stay
You've got to

His breath smelled while he pondered the verse over my shoulder.

"That's not bad," he said. "What about *in*-spire"

I gave it some thought and shook my head.

"*Per*-spire?"

"Uncle Lemmie," I rebuked him. "this is serious. I was down in the cellar before, and if they don't call the fire engines soon, we won't *have* a house. There's a whole pile of Daddy's old newspapers caught fire from the stove."

What with Daddy running with water buckets in a minute or two and Mommy screaming and Uncle Lemmie and my brother breaking the fire alarm box and calling the fire engines, and the firemen pulling hoses all over the porch, the poem never got finished. But when the firemen, chopping and dousing away, had saved about three-quarters of the house, Daddy said, "What the *hell* was she writing poetry for?" And Mother hit me hysterically in the back of the head and said, "Why didn't you tell us?" But even after Uncle Lemmie had explained about the rhyme, they didn't understand.

Now I believe the act of poetry is always utilitarian. For *them,* of course, my wanting to communicate in poetry at all, and my searching so hard for the perfect rhyme to do it with, remained –forever– a purpose mysterious, rankling, insolubly perverse. But that was because I never told them that it was I who had set the fire.

I was a fat little girl–wretchedly fat. In the photographs I have, I look blonde, bloated, and worried. There was so much of me that I thought I was a freak, and I was preoccupied with my physical being–in fact, my earliest memories are not of people at all, but sensations. A deeply buried excitement as of a smaller body within my own body, gradually expanding to giant proportions –that's the earliest. It happened only during absolute darkness, silence, rest, probably as I was falling asleep in my crib, and came of itself, like grace. Something within me formed and grew–swelling, swelling out of all belief, doubling, tripling the limits of my already puffed tiny body as I lay overpowered and rigid, exulting unpardonably in my size but helpless with the fear that any moment I would burst.

Another–a burning sensation which began in the mouth and ran quickly through the rest of me, inside and out, as though I were on fire–happened only once, I think, in infancy but recurred in later life quite often, in moments of feared passion, usually as a prelude to lovemaking. (According to my mother it can be traced back to my first summer, to the time my father drew the water for my bath. He had boiled the water on the stove and added it to the basin, assuming my mother would add cold as needed. She assumed that he had already adjusted the temperature. And proceeded to add me, instead. I screamed in time as my heel went in, and the result was only a kind of reverse Achilles' heel, a blister which became a permanent tough scar. But in my own opinion this episode can't account for the flaming sensation I remember, and later on have experienced again, since this always begins in the mouth.)

My father was a lawyer, a tiny man with a moustache that looked phony and big ears with tufts of hair growing in them. His voice was unbelievable. People who heard him speak for the first time, only a few words of trivial conversation, were invariably shocked: that out of such a tiny man, under the suddenly arched lip and moustache, broke a voice like an overloaded loudspeaker, metallic, compelling, and deeply annoying. Perhaps that was why his legal successes were cerebral ones, triumphs of the office rather than the court. Still, he believed with passion in forensic skill and he began training my older brother Sander from early childhood in public speaking–heading him for the bar and, I suppose, congress. He used to have Sandy stand up at the table after dinner every night to speak extemporaneously for five minutes to all of us (though Mother usually left in obvious boredom) on whatever topic my father chose. These were usually matters of childhood interest, though later, as Sandy grew older, they became wider in scope, political or philosophical. Often, however, they were topics of mere absurdity. Indeed my father claimed that–for practice–the best subjects in the world on which to sharpen the teeth of logic and persuasion were those to which no reasonable man could listen. They would serve Sandy later, he claimed, like the weights carried by the Spartans or the stones in Demosthenes' mouth.

I recall in particular one of the absurd topics on which Daddy insisted Sandy speak, because it made, at the time, an almost mystical impression on me. I was four years old and Sandy was nine and he spoke with all the eloquence he could muster (which by that time was plenty) on the proposition that the sun was really the moon. I listened with my cheek on the table. Sandy stood by his chair as usual, alternately leaning on the table with curled fingers and standing back from it, pushing the blond hair off his forehead, squinting one eye sometimes while he spoke, blowing his nose once or twice and picking it, and pointing a subtle finger at the moon. "You say you can see for yourself. But how good are your eyes? At that distance anyone could make a mistake, couldn't they? The evidence is suspicious right off. Even if every *one* of you thinks it's the sun, in China they all think they're standing on top of the world. And the earth looks flat, doesn't it? What we need is people with an open mind because the cards are stacked–"

"Facts," Daddy coached loudly, motioning with his toothpick at Sandy's pocket. "I have here."

"I have here reports from ten top scientists, disagreeing with each other about what the sun is made out of, and if those scientists can't agree, it's up to us. They say they have to look at it in an eclipse. Well, we ought to bring the thing down and have it looked at in broad daylight. And we could too, if they weren't spending all our money and keeping us cooling our heels out here in the outfield, trying to tell us what to do–"

"Drive it home!"

"It's up to every one of you to decide in his own heart. That poor moon might be up there all this time, every day, and everybody thinking it was the sun."

"No good," Daddy carped. "You missed the point: the sun *is* the moon."

I was shivering with attention and overwhelmed by what I had heard. Were they seriously proposing that the sun *was* the moon? Or were they proposing that the two ought to be changed, could be changed? I lay with my cheek on the table, rigid with wonder.

Though not the first, this was one of my earliest exposures to the idea of transformation, which as the critics have noted, recurs often in my poetry, and without which I would never have risked the daring realism of utterly transforming myself into what otherwise–for all the hacks and quacks around– would have remained only potential in me for a lifetime. "It's all relative" is the cant phrase you hear now even in grocery stores or on park benches. And "It's all in your point of view" –far too easy, isn't it, and any honest man, if pushed, will admit it's not quite true. One's point of view–the eyes of the beholder–can't *really* transform a thing. An additional step, a tougher and solider adventure is needed before you can have transmutation, or crime, or poetry.

In any case, for years, Sandy used to practice a rhetoric of sophistication and deceit (the kind he later used so successfully to have his way with me), while I listened, rapt with admiration and jealous of his skill and intelligence. I never managed to realize that the five years' difference in our ages, by which he kept exactly the same distance ahead of me all the time, had anything at all to do with it; he seemed unreachably brilliant and beautiful: his sharp features, his freckles, his skinny boy's body. I wanted his mind and body for my own. I raged and desired him unconditionally. And certainly no little girl's wishes were ever answered so unconditionally.

"You never know what's underneath," my father said to

quiet me. It's the very earliest memory I have of him. He had taken me to the matinee at a local theater one Saturday–a kind of vaudeville performance for children. On stage a troupe of dancing animals snarled back at the trainer's whip, and the audience of children was uneasy. "You never know," my father said, his hand on the back of my neck, soothingly. I was three and a half. When the biggest animal of all came down off the stage–a lion, I suppose, though to me he was only Animal–and began to climb through the theater over the empty rows up front, the children panicked. From where I sat toward the side, he seemed to be climbing over the audience, his paws on their heads. Still, I kept quiet. He came fourfootedly up the center aisle and paused, the audience shrieking and backing away. To calm them, he sat back on his haunches and proceeded to slit his throat, from his furry chin down–out came a man's head: I screamed–down to his groin: a man's body: I screamed louder.

What terrified me then, and always has, is not the beast in man, but the man in the beast. Look at the person nearest you this moment and you'll see what I mean. The emergence of man from animal is always half complete: I see him standing there, cheap actor, one leg out of the fur forever. Our history only repeats the first man's history. When he stepped out completely and shook the dead golden rag on the floor, I went wild. I screamed hysterically for almost ten minutes, my father trying to stop me in the lobby with loud, reasonable arguments. And let me mention that later on, one of the most soul-terrifying moments I've ever had (the resultant short poem, "Boy, You Theban Beast," is one of my most celebrated) came to me when I looked at my brother, then grown old, and saw that in fact he was not a beast.

My brother, five years more interested than I was in "what's underneath," took me under the bed one day when I was four and he was nine to find out. "Let's swap," he said. "You look, I look." I had no particular objection, but he added "Give and take, that's the way the world works." In the midst of a very thorough exploration, he announced himself disappointed. "What a gyp! This is no trade—there's nothing here."

I got quite used to this sort of examination in childhood. I underwent a number of them, and reactions were always the same. I always remained quite passive and uninterested myself. It was only the last, performed by a gynecologist when I was sixteen, which —as the reader will see—excited me, as Keats said of Cortez, with a vast surmise.

One apprentice publicityman offered in trade his really long appendicitis scar and I accepted. A group of robber barons stopped me in the park and offered to gouge and club me with the blades of their iceskates if I didn't immediately lift up my skirt and take down my pants. Their enthusiasm puzzled me. I considered refusing, because it was already getting dark, a late winter afternoon, and I was afraid I might be cold. But it seemed to me I recognized them. The bushes into which I had been pushed were part of the small park grounds of the Children's Museum, where I had gone with friends after school. After the others left, I had stayed behind to see an exhibition of sculpture and lantern slides about the facts of birth and anatomy, entitled "Natures Miracle." I had seen the same group of boys with iceskates in the auditorium, I knew. And though their approach was odd, the idea of being asked to take my small part in the exhibition of a miracle seemed reasonable. Patiently, I complied. One of the young toughs said wearily, "See, what'd I tell ya."

Mother raised a great cry when I told her. "Eight years old!" she wailed. She called Daddy at the office, but he wasn't in. Then she took me around the corner to the police station and raised a great cry there. I was staggered when we were given a patrol car and two policemen to search for the boys. We toured the neighborhood: I had been at ease in the park but I was frightened in the patrol car. We slowed up past every group of boys on the streets, especially those with iceskates, and I began to think it would soothe everybody if I merely pointed my finger at no matter whom. The policeman kept saying, "There, kid?" And my Mother kept threatening, "When I get my hands on them . . ." But looking closely, I saw that her eyes were shut, and this disturbed me. The odd part of this ride was that we actually did come across the boys—I recognized in particular the one who had insulted me by being bored with my miracle. But something about Mother's eyes being closed, as though upon her own private version of the deed, warned me and stopped me. I said nothing at all.

It was a habit of hers. She had large eyes, and she kept them closed a lot of the time, when she was playing the piano, or when she was just sitting, and under the taut lids you could see her eyeballs moving. I felt she was never of this moment or in this room. And then the upper surfaces of her forearms were covered with fine black hair; I used to struggle when she hugged me, as though I were being dragged backward in time against my will. Hugging me, she would tell me long stories of the slums in which she had lived as a girl until Daddy found her, of the nuns who gave cocoa and graham crackers to the girls every Wednesday, of the pitiful dresses she had had to wear. (She made lovely dresses for me, of taffeta and embroidered cotton, which crinoline slips often, and little aprons of which I was very proud, partly because I thought they helped hide my stout shape.) And we laughed regularly and immoderately together whenever she told me how she once spit from the third floor landing of a great marble library staircase onto the glittering bald pate of a gentleman in the lobby, because she admired its gleam so. At the "splat" of the hit, which sound she imitated, we shrieked.

There was a strange absence of logic in Mother, or the presence of a personal anti-logic, which appealed to me when I was extremely young, but which began to disturb me even by the time I was seven. Once, I recall, she was washing the dishes with her eyes closed and broke a plate; she walked across the room where Sandy was quietly reading, and slapped him hard, telling him he talked too much–which was certainly true.

I pondered Mother a long while, and more as I grew older. Father and Sandy trying with their arguments to sew up our daily life with the threads of persuasion; Father trying with his law practice to spin the affairs of men generally, and crime in particular, into a cocoon of rules and consequences; and Mother, with her eyes closed and a flick of her hand, destroying their webs. I have always pretended (even to myself) to be of Father's and Sandy's party, trying to trap life in the nets of my own reason and expression–especially in the poorer parts of my poetry–but I see now that I have been deeply and upsettingly committed to Mother all along. When

I wrote my first poem of warning and kept searching for the rhyme, I was only pretending to be on their side; I was on her side when I set fire to the house. But I'm not proud to admit it—because whenever I try to remember Mother, I see her in the patrol car, her eyelids gripped on revenge.

On the street all the way home from the police station she lept hugging me, every few feet; she kept it up even after we got home until I began to think that, without knowing it, I had really been injured in some way which she wouldn't tell me about. I began to cry. I was still crying when Daddy came home and we told him. He got incensed for awhile, and then relaxed into, "So they were checking on science, were they?" and finally concluded, "Boys will be boys." Mother was shocked. She wanted to alert the school authorities and the papers. But Daddy kept a calmer view. "Boys!" he boomed vastly, blotting out with that loud monosyllable all questions of right and wrong, blame or tears. "Kid stuff!" Sandy mimicked intensely, studying me.

It was about this time that I began to get a bit thinner—more boyish, I felt, with immense pleasure—and began to chase, in desperate tomboy style, after Sandy and his friends. Most of the time they managed to elude me, or they teased me with games that demanded feats physically impossible for me. One summer day, with me at the tag end, Sandy led the pack on a chase of Follow the Leader—jumping from high walls, swinging from trees, climbing over barbed wire fences. On the last of these I tore both the hem of my skirt and my calf: a ragged, bloody cut behind and below the knee. I still have the scar too. He took me back to the house and treated the wound with cotton and iodine while I sat and writhed in a chair in the living room. There was no one else at home. I still remember how dark the living room was with the blinds drawn, and the smell of iodine which I thought was the smell of my blood, and Sandy's blue hat which he had debonairly tossed under the piano after wiping his fingers all over it to get the blood off them. I was crying. To quiet me (I thought), he said anxiously, "Would you like me to show you what grownups do at night?"

I must have sensed that there was something wrong because I immediately began crying louder, quite deliberately. Obviously, however, he had already given his plans much thought. He replied as if I had raised an anticipated objection. Resourcefully, he began drying my eyes with my braids, "There, there. You're never too young to learn. You're a clever girl, but you lack initiative."

He was almost fourteen years old, and the power of his rhetoric was by now formidable. I made no attempt to engage in debate. I adjusted my skirt which he had raised much too high to treat my leg (I suddenly noticed), and I started putting on the sock and shoe which he had removed because they were wet with blood. "I want to go out again and play," I said.

"That's the trouble with you girls. You want to grow up to be wives and mothers without the responsibilities of training for a profession. No wonder so many of you fail. Until the day you marry, you refuse to start practicing. It's all play with you, isn't it? You've got to take your responsibilities more seriously."

The best I could manage was the childish "You think you're so smart, don't you!" But it was I who thought it, and a lot more: radiant with his messy blond hair tufted above his ears, enviably slender, and manly, and graceful, and above all earnest and sensitive–with shadowy eyes and encyclopedic lips. "My leg still hurts," I said.

Singlemindedly, he continued, "Where do you expect to learn–" this said scornfully–"from books, from hygiene classes, from pajama party bull sessions? There's no substitute, I tell you, for the school of hard knocks. Experience is the best teacher, and practice makes perfect."

"Let's go," I complained, because by now he had his hand under my skirt and I began to have the first clear idea of what we had been talking about. I got up.

"All right, Millie," he said gravely, "let's be realistic. How do you want to learn about this? From Mommy and Daddy?"

The thought was embarrassing. "I'm going out to play," I repeated.

"And when? Do you want to have to wait till you're my age to find out?" That really gave me pause: waiting five years seemed an unimaginable strain.

"And then do you want to have to learn from strangers?" He had obviously saved his trump for last. I thought of all the little boys of my acquaintance. "What do I have to do?" I said cautiously.

But for all his brave arguments, he had only mistiest ideas (I realized much later). In the darkness of the living room, standing and gyrating and almost hopping forward across the rug, we performed together a weird ritualistic dance, based on his strenuous imagination and the observation of dogs. This way and that he turned me, making certain piston-like motions of his own, which frightened me and left him confused, but pleased at his daring. Finally he tied my shoelace for me and picked up his hat and we went out to play Follow the Leader again with his friends.

That evening, while Mother changed the Band-Aid, he stayed in the room listening to see if I would say a word about what had happened, and we were both flushed the whole time. Still frightened, I said nothing. After dinner, at Daddy's suggestion, Sandy delivered a fervent oration on the topic, "Firecrackers in the Hands of Children."

Gradually from that day on I began to hate Mommy and Daddy for making no attempt to interfere with us or stop us. I never allowed myself to realize that it was I who prevented them with my utter silence—How could they expect *me* to tell them? I thought. The only attempt I did make to tell occurred the next morning: I set fire to the house—and more, I tried words too, the very best words I knew—

> *I want to tell you right away*
> *About a big red fire,*
> *That if you want the house to stay*
> *You've got to*

But nobody understood. So I abandoned poetry, and I didn't try again until my teens.

And so, from that rude beginning in the living room grew a strange and unexpected vine: a slow, childish, and extremely delicate courtship. Sandy, sensing my resistance, became hesitant in his attempts, almost meditative, as though considering my age and our relationship. ("Wouldn't it be easy for me, Millie," he said, "to abuse the trust of my little sister? We have to keep this on the highest plane.") Though I found his new interest in me repulsive, his words distracted me. Did they not ring out with the authority I associated with Daddy at the dinner table? The serpentine logic, the fluent nonsense, confused me. Once when I protested his unbuttoning the back of my dress he said bewilderingly, "Silence is the golden rule, remember? Do unto others silently–in ethics and in the deep moments." It seemed to me that I did remember something like that. Still I screamed–at half volume–and he desisted, commenting, "The exception proves the rule." It was all over my head.

But little by little as I realized the power I had over him, my ancient, poignant desire to have his sinuous mind and thin, freckled body for my own, and thus to triumph over him, seemed within reach. Though I was frightened, he was offering them to me–always tactful and considerate–"your respect, Millie, has to come first" –until I began both to want him and to love him as the World's Treasure. Yet so slow were we that we did not actually consummate our feelings for three years, until I was eleven, and even then it was a most gentle consummation, and certainly not a real penetration, partly because Sandy could never quite figure out how to manage, and partly because of my physical abnormality–of which more later.

Generally we waited until we were alone at home in the evening, which happened occasionally, and then I would shower or bathe, and Sandy would wash me. Or sometimes, even when my parents were home, I would go into his room and sit next to him while he studied his Latin or mathematics. You may doubt me when I say that he really studied, but he had great powers of concentration and won all sorts of school prizes in both Latin and mathematics, possibly because I encouraged his love for them. I came, in fact, to marvel at his capacity for simultaneous interest, the daring heights to which his intellectual and sexual excitement could hurl itself at both extremes, brain and groin (Quem ad finem sese effrenata iactabit audacia?). When in my later poetry or the very first few essays I've had occasion to write, I speak of "completing the man" or

> *The easy sweet of the banana*
> *Split: ends of herself in heaven and hell*
> *Bent double*

I think back to the evenings with Sandy. Searching in his clothes with love, I felt that I helped to create, at least in its more godly aspect, his sexual organ. Even today, I don't think I was really wrong about that. Some of the bewildering enigmas about how things get created—both in the universe of physics and in that of art—later seemed clearer to me: the tense forces released in the approach and separation of opposites; the paralyzed shimmering when they are put unstably together. But for the reader who may remain shocked, despite all philosophical reflection, by the story of my brother and me, I'll add—for your most serious consideration—that it was precisely these years of incest which in the long run kept me from the terrible perversions of homosexuality.

During this period, my face thinned, my features became clear and delicate, my body lengthened. Unreasonably, I suspected that I owed all of these changes to Sandy, as though by his attentions he had given me a new physical being. My gratitude was inwardly slavish. I thought of very little else except of him. I was utterly uninterested in school, other girls, boys. Only the things Sandy said to me seemed important, though I must admit that that was partly because they seemed mysterious. Once he rattled off: "Politics makes strange bedfellows, too. But there's something very satisfying about that. After all, we need the illusion of democracy, though I suppose it's only a question of whether we want to be ruled by the same few or a changing few." He was tucking me in for the night at the time, I didn't sleep for hours, puzzling over what he meant.

Another evening, while he was working away at his biology assignment, I remember that he commented, "We are just the beginning, you and I, the single cell. We're the binary fission of ourselves, out of which will later come the more highly developed forms of life and specialized reproduction."

I never forgave him for going away to college. I was desolate. But the night before he left he sneaked into my room, and for the first time we spent the entire night cushioned together, like two Egyptian brother-sister princelings in a temple over the Nile, watching the river of clouds thought my window–tearless and serious and dignified at parting, as befits royalty. "Since I'm going away," Sandy must out loud in his endless peroration, "let's make it an entering wedge. It has to stop some time–"

"Does it? There'll be summers."

"No. it has to stop. Millie, you're going to become a woman–"

"Will I?" I said wistfully. I was almost thirteen.

"Of course. We'll be man and woman, grown and separate. And I suppose we'll be embarrassed when we look back, but let's not regret it. After all, we made the choice. Now we've got to make other choices–"

"Construct other choices," I corrected him ironically–the first time it had ever entered my head to correct him, or to be ironical.

I was awed at myself.

Desperately, I began writing verse again–filled a while year's diary with girlish love poem, pleading with him for his affection. Impatiently I kept waiting for his first summer vacation. But he was as good as his word and when he did come back, he remained irreproachable, unapproachable. After he left again for the second year, I succumbed to endless nighttime imaginings of his presence in my bed.

With a good deal less interest I kept waiting to become a woman, as a kind of consolation, never forgetting that Sandy had seemed to promise it to me. I was already rather pretty, blonde and graceful, and as thin as a young girl should be. But I was worried because by that time I should also have been adolescent. I began to think that nature was spitefully withholding my maturity from me on account of my precocious adventures with my brother. I was already fourteen and terribly conscious whenever I undressed with the other girls during swimming periods at the school that I was childishly hairless and flatchested. It seemed to me that for purely physical and therefore unfair reasons, the other girls were automatically relegating me to the position of social failure; I resented it.

When Sandy came home the second summer, I consulted him, hoping almost to tempt him by making him touch me where I was flat. Mocking me goodnaturedly, he said, "Let's construct a choice for you, Millie." So he carved a pair of sponged into the proper shape, and when school came round again in the fall, on his advice I dropped swimming classes and began wearing my womanhood inside a brassiere. The result was immediate and it shocked me: I had more invitations than I could accept. Since except Sandy, I wanted to keep the boys at a far distance but at the same time wanted the appearance of social success, the solution was painless. Of course whenever I was taken to the movies I was dreadfully afraid of detection all the time and went so far as to dip the points of the sponges into a bit of mucilage, which then soaked up and hardened inside the sponge like nipples. Although the imitation was hardly accurate, the boys, in their ignorance, accepted it gladly, and in the darkness they pressed and compressed the sponges until they exhausted themselves, while I enjoyed the evening in perfect freedom, sensationless. When a hand strayed to my leg, an occasional slap on the wrist was all that was needed; they returned happily to what I was willing to give. In that way for sometime I enjoyed my triumph—as word spread among the boys at school—without yielding one breath of my devotion to Sandy.

In fact, I was well over sixteen before my breasts began to come up naturally—small and soft and perfect, just as they should have been, I supposed—but at the same time a fine blonde down began to come out on my face. At first it was only on the upper lip, then later on the cheeks and chin, but I began to have visions of becoming the bearded lady of the circus, as my earliest fears of being a freak were revived. I wanted to shave off the down; but Mother said that that would only encourage it, and sent me to a doctor. The doctor said it might pass of itself, but if it didn't, he could take the hairs out electrically. At first I refused to consider that. But when my voice began to get distinctly hoarse and a bit foggy, so that I began to be noticed with laughter at school and even Daddy made fun of me sometimes, booming out at me with that exploding voice of his, I went into virtual seclusion for a time, trying to decide. Mortified, I pleaded the onset of painful menstruation—which was utterly untrue. But with a little modest artifice here, too, I even convinced Mother.

I stayed in the bedroom for almost seven days, meditating and deciphering. It seemed to me clear that nature was at last completing its vendetta against incest, and that I had been selected as the object of a monstrous sexual revenge. The more I thought, the more certain it seemed. But I determined to consult a specialist.

Pleading continued illness, I persuaded Mother to make an appointment with a gynecologist; in order to go alone, I called the doctor secretly, changed the time of the appointment, from afternoon to morning. When mother was out, I dressed, trying to make myself look as mature and feminine as possible. I chose my most daring dress, I put on silk stockings and heels, I pinned up my hair, and I wore a little hat of Mother's with a blue dotted veil.

At the doctor's I was earnest and decorous, confident of the effect of my clothes. At first, the doctor himself struck me as a dapper salesman, a smooth-talking hawker; later, during the examination, he struck me as a brute. Without the slightest consideration for the embarrassed feelings of a sixteen-year-old girl in her first pelvic examination, he treated me as he would have treated any other patient. But when

I was ready, reclining on the table with my knees wide, I realized that there could be no mistake, and the thought comforted me with the promise of finality. The doctor was saying, "Nothing to worry about if a girl matures late . . . yes, there *is* some underdevelopments here . . . arrested uterus . . ."

He sat down suddenly and put his had over his heart.

"Am I all right, doctor?" I said, afraid to move. "Or am I a boy?" It was more than a question–it was a chorus of conviction.

"Don't move, Miss," he said, short of breath, as if he thought I were going to fade like a miracle. And in a moment he was back to the examination, palpating my abdomen.

Doctors all over the country soon became familiar with the details of my case, since several studies of my anatomy subsequently appeared in the *Journal of the American Medical Association* as well as other medical publications in Britain and America. Briefly, the medical picture was this: not only did I have the female organs with which I had been born, still in infantile condition; I also had, retracted and sealed in vaginal tissue, the organs of the male sex, by now fully adolescent and, so to speak, trapped. As the doctor himself put it, moments after he had finished examining me, "You're not a boy Miss," and he was sweating when he said it.

"You're also a boy."

For weeks, specialists examined my "miracle." I was, they told me, a true hermaphrodite, a "genetic accident" known not only to the annals of modern science, but known form the testimonies of ancient art and literature to have appeared now and again throughout history and all over the world. But today, they said, it was another matter. In our society a true hermaphrodite was impermissible–and besides, correctable. The two possibilities were clear. Would I like to have my newfound male organs cut away surgically, and my female organs brought to full maturity with hormones? Or conversely: would I like to have my manly parts released to their normal position, and my uterus and ovaries cut away? "It's up to you Millie." Me? "You or your parents," they said. "Take your choice–male or female."

Although the full complexities were not clear to me for weeks, still, even in those first ten minutes after I learned the truth, I realized that I was a lot less confused than the doctor; all my experience had made it possible for me to grasp without vertigo the news of my sexual fusion. I had the uncanny impression that I had actually transformed myself–into a freak, if you will–by an alchemy of illicit desire. And that I was now hopelessly triumphant: I was to be deprived of Sandy forever. Getting dressed again in the doctor's office, fixing the garters to my silk stockings and slipping my heels back on, I began to search for a way back.

That same night, I discussed the doctor's visit with my shaken parents for five difficult hours. Daddy's voice seemed to lose its spring; his steeltrap mind opened limply, "Millie darling," he whispered, "you won't let them . . . alter you . . . would you?" I vowed in a horrified baritone that I wouldn't let them take my womb. Fiercely, Mother kept sobbing, "We'll sue the doctor." They phoned. They hung up. Unanimously and desperately they pleaded with me to remain their daughter. But I will say this to their credit: they left the choice to me.

I said goodnight– for the first time without kissing them– and went to bed. I sat on the edge. I had equaled Sandy, and in doing so, lost him. But it wasn't irreversible. I slipped off my heels–unhooked my garters–pulled down one stocking–and instead of going to sleep, took up a pencil. The words, the lines, seemed to force themselves lovingly on me, as if I had to hold my twin self visibly at arm's length from me on paper to decide. It was the work of a sixteen year old girlboy, addressed to her lost-and-found brother.

> *Out of the sun I lived with you in trust*
> *A double son in dark might each be proud,*
> *Revolve in you (my girlish moon must*
> *Fold its song, no longer loud)*
> *Serene your single orbit bring me birth.*
> *But now my spectral dust*
> *To dust–and yours the mirth–*
> *Must quite alone unwind its shroud*
> *And bring a squeaking man on earth.*

It was almost light when I woke up. I read the lines over several times, and saw that I had decided. I had chosen, at the very least, to become a poet. I would have to learn to seem outwardly beyond the reach of doubt–daring, energetic, and perhaps (to be absolutely safe) coarse. With the disguise of surgery, I could parade my hard-won maleness. But for myself–with poetry as my ruse and my salvation–I would keep my double sex physically intact. A public man with a private womb. My transmutation, my twinning–I would not give up one iota.

Willy Nilly

Sentimentally, I've kept a bulging manila envelope full of pictures from that far-off time. Candid camera shots of me smirking on the porch, flashbulb snaps of me gobbling at Thanksgiving dinner. When I pulled the rubber band off the envelope, I experience an unpleasant twinge in my groin. There I stand with a skirt on–in several photos you can even see the beginnings of my girlshape under my blouse. In others taken only months later, I'm wearing pants and a tie, looking skinny and afraid. There's one eloquent photograph: it's a group picture and it tells the story; we're all standing there, Mother's fists and eyes grimly clenched, Father's tongue proudly flexing his moustache, and my brother Sandy's fingers gingerly clasping my shoulder. I'm the blonde sixteen-year-old lad up front with the bright embarrassed teeth.

To comprehend any sexual situation, you really ought to see the before-and-after shots of my operation. The medical close-ups of my naked saddle–these are fascinating. Every detail of my genitals, exposed during and after surgery to the most expensive medical photographic equipment, shows with clarity on this expert series of stills depicting my transformation from girlhood to manhood. It's almost too graphic for words: below my *mons veneris* emerges first the *glans* of my penis, then gradually the shaft; then in the place of my girl-lips appear (photographed in four stages of emergence) my testicles. The successful procedure adopted by the surgeon was at once featured in medical journals here and abroad.

But beforehand, I must admit, I'd had my doubts. "Are you kidding?" I said. "Life is real, life is earnest–"

"Miss"–the surgeon scrutinized my face–"this not a matter for jokes or a time for poetry." He made an indelicate pun about Longfellow, which I won't bother to repeat. "You will be able to function well and normally. Still, what you don't or won't understand is that even after I've completed your first operation, you'll still have the gonads of both sexes–ovaries and testes–unless I operate *further*. Now I've explained this twice to your father and mother–I will not take responsibility for the case otherwise–I refuse to help you out of your remarkable situation–until I have obtained your consent to a second operation, Miss. And to avoid the possibility of doubts… ambiguities…"–he leaned forward and placed a stubby fingertip on the belly of slacks I was wearing–"and shadows, I want to remove your ovaries."

Medical science is clearheaded, He tapped. He showed me firmly where he wanted to go in. He frightened me… of course he did… but I didn't lose my wits. I could be firm, too, and just as clearheaded. What did he expect me to do? I didn't want to be a Longfellow. I was sixteen and stubborn about my body. And passionately patient. I explained to the blunt-fingered surgeon, to the rest of the medical world, and to my baffled parents how enormously grateful, how glad I'd be, to become male–physically, mentally, emotionally–the works. But, I cried out, I didn't want to have my ovaries and womb touched, cut out–good God! They were *my body*–couldn't they understand that?–I wanted them left where they were, only sealed off, made impossible for legal purposes (Father's idea) and impassable for practical purposes (mine). Thoroughly unusable, but *there*, not taken away. And I even explained why at home. "For black and white, for silver and gold, for sun and moon."

Father had a good mind, but he was no help at all. He flushed, controlling his anger and confusion. "There's not going to be any gray in this house, no girlish boys in *my* family, you get that straight right now, once for all. For sixteen years we thought you were a girl. Okay. Anyone can make a mistake, Then out of the blue this lousy gynecologist discovers you're a genetic marvel. Well, grin and bear it–hermaphrodite–who even knew how to spell it? And now you turn around and tell us you'd rather be a boy–okay. It's your choice. So far, so good. But take your choice and abide by it: black or white. Even biological accidents have to be straightened out, Milly… an open-and-shut case." And suddenly without warning he broke down, "I can't stand it!" and roared, "Either–or! You hear me? You can't be both!"

"I am both."

"Then cut it out, you hear! You just cut this funny business out!"

"It's my funny business."

For the first time, the only time, he hit me–a swinging blow to the side of my head. I didn't believe the pain or where it had come from. My head heated up and I stared. The tears came.

Mother intervened, clasping me to her breast.

To Father, "You!" she said, "moron." To me, "Dear," she said for solace, "remember, no matter what happens, no matter what they do to you, you'll always be my little darling."

I unzipped my way out of her arms.

"Mother–"

But she only shook her head, closed her eyes. I was staggered. She hadn't even grasped my decision yet. Or else she had grasped it fully, more deeply than anyone else. In either case, argument was futile.

"The shilly-shallying," Father shouted, "is over! It's elementary logic! Simple LOGIC!"

But for all his noise he couldn't persuade Mother. Mother demurred, muttering, "On her birth certificate is says. Definitely. Signed and stamped. That's a government document, and it's *official*. I'm no dope, I'm nobody's sucker, so don't you worry."

On the floor–where else was I supposed to sink?–I said in tears, "Mother, stop."

"I brought you into the world. Girl! Who should know better? I washed you where it counts. Girl! I changed your diapers more times every day than jack Robinson could jump up a beanstalk. Girl!"

"Boy," I wailed.

"Now? Now after sixteen years you tell me?" She came close and she actually kicked me–right there on the ground where I was lying huddled up–several good kicks.

"I hate you both!" naturally I said.

"You double-crosser!" Mother flashed, breathing her gold fillings at me.

Families never understand, Even my gynecologist was kinder. "Milly dear, no one's going to force you against your will, but why don't you give in? Don't you see that this misunderstanding, this extraordinary stubbornness of yours, is pure fright—hysteria in every sense of the word? It's true that you were born a hermaphrodite. That's not your fault. And it's true that if you absolutely insist, we can leave your womb intact. But it's going to atrophy anyway. After the second operation, your entire female system is going to waster away even if we don't touch it. Wither. Poof! Gone anyhow, You're going to be a boy, Milly."

In fact, as soon as I came to realize, I held the trumps. The one trump. It was in me. None of the doctors who were brought into the case could tolerate the thought of simply leaving me as I was. Their minds boggled at it—letting me remain a girl, sexually infantile?—when right there, buried behind a tiny wall of tissue and growing every day I had an adult male phallus?

"Easier than a nose job," the surgeon assured me, cheering me on while the nurses who had just prepped me wheeled me through the corridors into the elevator. In the operating room I had a few moments of paralyzing doubt and terror: bending over me, the surgeon winked.

"A stiff upper lip, kid," he said next morning, winking past on his hospital rounds. I'll see you again in a couple of months for the rest of the work."

For a time I was dizzy, sick from the after-effects of anesthesia and feverish with a sense of anticipation, It must have been the second day when Father came to visit and cried, putting his head on the foot of my bed, The third or fourth day, as soon as the ache in my groin was bearable, I stood up, without the nurse's permission, staggered gingerly into the bathroom, and locked myself in. Half a week after the operation, the bandages had been partially loosened: cautiously, I took them aside completely and– with my heart doing little scared squirrel jumps between my two tiny fluttery breasts–I examined myself.

There! God Almighty! There it hung! My swinger! Frankly, I'll admit to you I'd expected something–well, heavier, wealthier, more muscular, more dramatic, (I'd only seen my brother Sandy's grand organ erected.) This one looked a trifle on the unambitious side. Still, even a hungry, skinny one was a grand one, I decided optimistically, And right there underneath… yes, that funny little fleshy sac of testicles. Only then did I come to appreciate the surgical skill that had made my miracle a reality: when my pale brown hair grew in again, my curls would conceal the stitches; underneath, my familiar cleft was thoroughly blocked and hidden by the folds of the brave new sac. Only a scar was visible there, I satisfied myself that I was unenterable and undetectable unless you were a doctor who knew in advance the mystery of my locked compartment.

You know what I did next? I swung. I swung myself for the pure innocent unexampled pleasure of seeing my own tiny majesty swing Then I commanded him to RISE! He wouldn't, of course. Well, no matter. When I got back into bed, I was giggling with happiness.

All in all, I made a good-looking boy. A scrawny blue-eyed

blond kid. At home, under hormone treatment, in a matter of only a few weeks, my little breasts (which Mother and I called my "boobles") dwindled like two swollen bruises and soon receded altogether into my chest. I was deeply impressed by the mysteries of chemistry. Scissors, shears, knives–cutting my hair, clipping my nails, learning to play mumblety-peg, snipping loose threads from my underwear, which had to be perfect. I felt peculiar, pulling myself into boy's underwear.

I was under doctors' orders not to stimulate myself. Don't fret, they explained. Several months would have to elapse before the supporting tissues where the internal sutures had been placed would be fully healed, strong enough and secure enough to withstand certain natural strains. If erection occurred while I was asleep (it never did) or occurred by itself somehow (it simply wouldn't), I was not to worry. But under no circumstances was I to masturbate. Well, naturally I got impatient, naturally I worried, inevitably I fretted. Why no stirrings down below? Why no life, no quickening? Was it because I was too small? *Was* I too small? It wasn't that I wanted to masturbate. No–but I wanted to grow. I pinched and I pushed and I pulled and *once*, once I got my limp member, my absurdly pink delicate resisting flesh, out to a maximum extension of two inches. I could claim no special knowledge of the field, but my two flaccid inches struck me as undersized.

Still, I was reasonably confident. I knew it would take time. To measure my progress accurately, I hid the garage. I took my notebook with me and a yardstick. And I can't tell you how tragic I felt when, no matter how I tried, I didn't, I couldn't, it wouldn't. It was dim in there and quiet. Father's car was gone, but the place smelled of gasoline, oil, rust. There were rags, tools, sparkplugs. How? In God's name, how? I rubbed, I massaged, I jumped… how did one make it rise?... surely by some physical means. Or maybe by thought? Do you believe in making physical things rise by thought? I didn't, but I knew I had to be open-minded in a field where a girl's experience was irrelevant. All right–levitation, then. I tried thinking about women. I tried movie actresses, I confess I even tried my mother, I tried the bodies of girls down the block, No good, no use, no luck. Well, after all, I knew logically that after sixteen years of being a girl I'd stand a greater chance of success if I thought of boys, or if I remembered precisely how it had been in bed with my brother Sandy kissing and holding me, but I absolutely *would* not, good Lord! I'd resolved to become a boy, a normal boy. Not even for the purpose of masturbation could I entertain for one minute the idea of homosexual incest.

Funereally, head hanging, I returned to my bedroom Some people might have been permanently flattened by a disaster like this. Not me. I've always had that saving streak, that old American stick-to-itiveness. It was Booker T. Washington, I think, who said wisely that you should judge a man, not by the heights to which he has risen, but by the depths from which he has come.

I cut up another sheet of heavy cardboard. I made five big white squares, and on those squares I printed in darkest India ink the indelible letters of my ineradicable name–

MILLY

—one letter to a square. I spaced those five squares along the wall, tacking them in a row over my bed, then out into the kitchen, and from the top of the refrigerator I took down the wishbone–drying there since the Sunday before my operation. And I broke it with Mother. I used Sandy's trick, the upper thumb. So I won. "Brat," Mother muttered, "I suppose you think you're going to get out of washing the dishes now?" and she threatened me with her thumb, jerking it toward… "Take the garbage out!" Ignoring her, I locked my bedroom door, hid the larger jagged piece of the wishbone under my pillow, and stood in front of my mystic sign, hands clasped over my new-found jagged sexual organ. I shut my eyes and wished, wished harder, harder. I reached for the wall and flicked the first letter upside down. Eyes open.

WILLY

There I was! Proceeding according to plan, with my left hand I rubbed my organ zealously–it wouldn't grow or rise, I knew, but it tingled–I rubbed until I felt the wall In front of me vibrating with my own impassioned energy and essence. I concentrated all my force. With my right hand I spun my first letter, I had taken care to tack it loosely, the better to spin it.

Round and round my letter spun. I watched–sure of it. Spinning, it came up W, nine times out of ten.

Every day I traveled by trolley car across the city to a new school–it was a sensible arrangement, Father's idea. He was all for being positive and thoroughgoing about change. And unlike Mother, he'd accepted me immediately. My sensitive nostalgia, my holding on to a few of my old inner organs, remained a mystery to him; still, I'd chosen to become a boy, I'd jumped the fence. He jumped with me and began thumping me on the back the way he used to thump Sandy. "Let 'em know who you are," he'd say every morning as I left for school. But I was just as glad that nobody cared (only the principal had been informed). To the teachers, to the other pupils, I was just another nuisance–a boy who'd somehow go transferred in the middle of the term–a new, pale, scared kid in the lower senior class. I was scared because from the start I was physically intimidated. The involuted psychological warfare by which girls maintain their power circles may be more cruel than the direct approach of boys, but the latter scared me half out of my wits. I hadn't been there a week before I got picked on. A lanky boy with eyes that were watering under his glasses shoved me sideways for no reason, so that I hit the wall and fell. As I fell he jammed his elbow into my ribs. I had a raspberry on my shoulder and a black-and-blue mark on my ribs for the next week. I was so paralyzed with fright I didn't even cry.

"I'm leaving school," I wailed to Father when he came home that evening. "I can't stand it."

"Good," he said. "A little fast, but it's the lesson you've got to learn."

Furious with him, I started to walk out of the room–but he held on to my arm. "You've got to stand up to them."

Mother nearly screeched, "Fight back? I don't want her fighting with boys."

I gave her a dirty look for the pronoun, but I felt the same way myself. "I'm not fighting with anyone."

"You don't have to fight if you know how to stand up to them."

"All I want is to be treated with a little consideration."

"Then you should have stayed a girl."

"Boys are animals," I shouted. "I'm not, and I'm not going to become one."

But Father had already begun looking up jiu-jitsu in the classified telephone directory.

At first the shock of physical combat with a man—the instructor, a balding Japanese perfectionist named Haidu—actually made me cry. I wept, but instead of pausing to console me, he bounded into the air, coming at me with both feet forward: I was so shocked I defended myself. "No that way. You this way," he said, holding me upright with his feet, then sitting up like a bolt and seesawing me across his forearm. When I made a mistake he hissed.

For over a month, Haidu's jack-in-the-box tactics, the smell and clumsiness of his pupils, the constant touch of the sweating half-naked struggling bodies of the other boys in the class, revolted and horrified me. But I was mesmerized by a motive, an idea, that would never have occurred to Father, Physical prowess—confidence in my body—I would, I thought, soon tighten the psychic springs, the springs that caused a member to grow taut and potent.

I wanted to learn, I used to watch with awe at the very beginning of every class for the first sight of Haidu coming through the door like a tubby oriental Superman, his kimono billowing behind him and his tights too tight. He looked funny, but in motion his body was ferocious. It frightened me until I discovered that—no matter how violent or stunning his gymnastics—all the while his face preserved a kindly, doll-gentle, distant look. So I tried to concentrate on his face, to see nothing but that gentle look of his even when he was springing at me, and this maneuver actually helped me. Slowly, and with practice, my timing became perfect. I began to get at least the elementary exercises and responses down pat—provided I was working out with Haidu himself. The moment he paired me with one of the sweaty boys in class, I fumbled badly.

One evening Haidu detained me after class. "Too much restraint," he said, hissing. I had no idea what he meant, but I felt miserable. "Woman is restraint," he continued. "Man is energy." Observing the bright, babylike look in his eyes, I had the tearful impulse to confide in him. But I restrained the impulse and stood there, hesitating for words. He waited for me to speak. When I said nothing, he repeated, "Too much restraint," and walked out of the room.

For weeks thereafter I worked like a demon. I would become Energy Incarnate. It went so far that Haidu suddenly had to hiss at me, with a wink, "More restraint, Hishi." Had he discovered something? He began using the new nickname, always with a wink, and taking special care with my progress. It was as if he had adopted me as his protégé. I complained to him that I was too light; he showed me how to use a stronger or heavier opponent's power as though it were my own, by pivoting against it to change its direction and adding its new direction to my own. "Take care, Hishi," he said, winking, "and you will become perfect instrument. You have secret already in own body. What is art of judo? It is balance point of restraint and energy, Shift balance suddenly, and you have attacked. Remove restraint, and attacker's energy will lose force."

Once, when I ended someone's knife charge too abruptly by knocking the rubber knife out of his hand instead of seizing his wrist, Haidu reproved me, shrilling, "Do no try to win, Hishi. Judo must be dance, not struggle, even when attacker thinks it is struggle. There is no opponent, only partner. Follow partner, and you will have victory without trying."

But on this score I was a bad pupil. I kept trying. I *wanted* to win. When I realized that a good intuitive sense of timing (which I had) was more important than strength, I learned to throw boys twice my weight, and the power to pinion a boy or to make him wheel over my arm or around me as a matador controls the bull had a tonic effect. I began to enjoy dominating boys, and–less frequently being dominated. Partly this was because I never quite got over the feeling that I was a kind of star-girl athlete, the kind that I have personally always detested. I couldn't help feeling that I was only play-acting the part of a boy, that under my trousers or gym shorts my doggy genitals were only sewed onto my crotch. To overcome my uneasiness, I used to force myself to parade naked in the locker room. This was almost unbearably difficult for me.

Father, of course, was delighted with my progress. "Aren't you glad you began jiujitsu?" he demanded, strutting up and down the living room.

"Golly, I sure am!"

His face changed sternly. "You've still got a lot to learn," he said, "a hell of a lot more. How to swear, for instance, and hot to walk like a boy, and…"

"And what?" I thought I might ask him for advice about self-stimulation. But there was no telling how he'd take it. I hesitated.

"Forget it… start with swearing," he said.

"Teach me."

The top of his forehead turned a dark red. "A boy doesn't ask his old man to teach him to swear. What you do is keep your ears wide open, you'll pick it up."

"Okay." I couldn't see why he was so grudging about it. But anything with words I could probaby manage to learn by myself. "What else?" I asked. He hesitated, thinking, which made his moustache tremble. I wondered if I should grow a moustache.

"It's not a question of *what else*, Willy–there isn't any next. It's all in your mental attitude. Being a man comes from inside you."

"Right." I made a mental note. "But you could try to be more helpful, Father. After all, I'm a late bloomer."

"Stop calling me Father"–his moustache twitched again. Was he going to laugh or cry? "Call me Pop."

"Okay, but I could use a few hints. What else?"

"Pop." He insisted.

"What *else, please!*" How could he expect me to call him Pop? Pop?

"Lots of things. Lots, kid. Most important, you got to learn…" He paused. He twitched.

I guessed. Squeezing my knees together hard, I forced it out. I said it, I was so proud of myself. "To jerk off, Pop?"

His perpetually open mouth slowly glided to a slit, stern and appraising. "No. That's on the docket for tomorrow, and don't you be wise with me. First things first. Listen, Willy"–it was very hard for him– "Willy, have you ever felt–maybe you already know what I mean–a certain attraction for the girls?"

It was hard for both of us.

I blushed and blushed.

He twitched and twisted. "Attraction comes first."

I studied attraction.

At school I sat in class studying girls. (My grades were lower than usual that year, except for French.) I hadn't the slightest idea how to begin. I suppose attraction does come first, but most boys begin very early with their mothers. In my case, that was out of the question. I thought of the few girls in my neighborhood who'd once been vague girl friends of mine, and I panicked. But now, what with buttoning my trousers every morning, eating hormones with my cereal, and trekking to the big school where there were hundreds of new junior and senior coeds around me, I figured I had a chance. I sat through history, math, English, study hall, lunch, biology, French, and physics, picking different magnets to stare at, trying out different positions in my seat, waiting for it to happen. Even an itch inside when I examined a girl's hemline would have felt like progress. But how? But when? The gynecologist and the clinical psychologist kept on claiming that there was nothing wrong with me organically; the problem, they said, was mental.

Naturally, I asked the doctors questions. By now, they said, tumescence should be a distinct possibility. Had I had any wet dreams as yet? Had I experienced any waking urges?

There was no hurry, they said. But there was. I asked every doctor I saw (and on routine check-up visits to the hospital I saw plenty) the most elementary questions. What *was* desire? What *caused* erection? And I got plenty of answers, elementary and complex: instinct, procreation, love, and sphincters. None of the answers helped a bit. The trouble down below was up above: there was a roadblock in my head. I tried to unblock.

"Sss!" There was a stocky boy named Dave who used to sit in front of me in history. Practically every day halfway through the class, I began to notice, he'd shift around in his seat, nudge his friend—"Ssss!"—and motion slyly with his eyes only—"Ssss!"—to the back of the room. She wasn't especially good-looking. But whenever Dave would signal, she'd be sitting there with her skirt up and her knees apart. It was the repetition that upset me. That young men of my own age should remain interested, every day and day after day, in the insides of a girl's thighs struck me as offensive and highly immature.

Still and all, transformation was possible—no one knew that better than I. So I determined to bend my whole will to the effort.

No one who has been only a boy can appreciate the enormous concentration with which I went about this monkey-imitation—how much it meant to me—and how nearly I succeeded. *Not* perfectly, no, but it was fine job on the surface. I hung around mainly on the school steps and in the candy store a block away. Every day I played the pinball machines, I read the comics, and I listened. I wrote everything down afterward, right away, and I made sure by practice that I could use every bit. I studied: the lingo, the gift of slow gab, the sullenness, the blinking. I was still a bit soft in the voce and skin, a trifle "boyish"–but it was hard to tell me from the real thing. Tough? I looked as if I *might* be, there on the outside–a sort of pallid-complexioned, too good-looking, even slightly feminine-looking punk was the effect I was aiming at, because it was all I dared hope for as yet. I hardly dared to believe that I was getting coarse on the inside. Yet sometimes it did seem to me that I scared some of my teachers when I entered a room just the right number of seconds late, slinked into a corner seat, and practiced staring at the radiator for forty minutes. But I couldn't be sure–maybe they were only worried about me.

I worked along several lines at once. I tried everything. After school, standing in the center safety strip of the big boulevard in our neighborhood, I practiced swearing. I swore at unsuspecting drivers, passed, passing, and to come. At first my tongue absolutely refused to produce the necessary sounds, so I would limber up on tongue-twisters at the beginning of each session. "Thelonious Throstle, the Thessalonian thistle sifter, sifted thistles with his thick thumbs." Then with my tongue still leaping, I'd take a running leap into four-letter words. "How much good would a good shmuck fuck if a good schmuck could fuck good." I exercised constantly, striving for easy expertise. "She smells pee smells by the wee whore." Difficult as it was, I invented fresh filth daily. "Peter Piper pecked his pick of speckled peckers." Yes, these were in terrible taste, but as I soiled my tongue, I polished my art.

I tired pornography, but all I could manage to get hold of were French pamphlets. The cartoons inside were absurd, and the text–well, I quickly discovered that French is simply not exciting. I buckled down hard to the problems posed by translation, but every time she'd open her *cuisses*, I'd have to start turning the pages of the dictionary. This is unnatural and distracting. She'd undo his buttons, she'd take his strong round white throbbing *cou* in both her hands, I'd race hopefully over to the *c*'s, down the columns, turn the page. For Godsake–his neck?! Besides, you know how it is: the crucial words weren't even defined by the dictionaries. You had to be a past master of the French language to have an erection.

I even tried dating. Only once. I asked a girl in my French class out to a movie. I'd been to the movies with girls before, when I'd been a girl (and with boys), but it gave me palpitations to ddo it again the new way. By now, however, I was desperate enough to try anything. In the flickering dark of the theater I tried everything. *"Mamelles, tètons,"* I whispered. She didn't respond. *"Viy,"* I murmured. I was unsure of certain distinctions, but I tried them all. *"Con, cul, cou, cuisses, couillons."* My entire repertory. She was a very unresponsive girl.

I began to doubt that she knew much French. But I didn't give up easily. I considered the possibility of tickling her arm, but thought I'd better work myself up into some semblance of desire first. I put one finger tentatively on the vegetable structure of her ear. And then, possessed by a suicidal heroism, forcing my courage by an exercise of will power, shutting my eyes tight, I reached out and did what you were supposed to do–I seized her by the breast. I held on manfully. I was sure she'd resist, but she didn't, she cooperated. It was awful. She moved toward me, settling lower in her seat, so I was left with this entire breast resting on my hand. Through the next few minutes I suffered. Her bosom was huge, resilient. Unwilling to be guilty of cowardice, I kept my fingers active. And all the while I sat there squirming with the intense pangs of jealousy–a throwback to the time I'd resented all breasts because I was flatchested.

I tried walking. After school one day I took a good square look at myself in the mirror, the large gold-framed mirror we had in the living room. There was no doubt about it. The reflection–the past in the present imperfect–depressed me. Those big eyes, owlish and frightened. A bird in a log, a girl's hanky soul in a boy's lanky body. I tried thumbing my nose at myself, but my eyes never got less sad. I tried walking around. It was true, as Pop said, my walk was wrong. All this paraphernalia of mine–my clipped boy's hair, collar, tie, belt, fly, crease, cuffs–only made my familiar girlish walk look worse. But I was determined, I was highly motivated. A proper boys' walk, I imagined, produced a natural stimulus: all day long his organ swung gently back and forth, constantly stirring his desire without resort to pornography. Sitting on school steps and park benches, analyzing various types of male strides, I decided that Father was right. I decided that although each boy had a different rhythm and energy, all had one thing in common: the splendid bright play of their shoulders, wrists, and knees came from inside out, from the center, the swinging pendulum of manhood. I took incredible pains to get it right.

All these workouts taught me the value of discipline. They strengthened my resolve, unlimbered my joints, and unlocked my throat. Pretty soon I could walk like a trooper and swear a mound of dung. In a couple of months, I'd outstripped Father's wildest hopes for me. So when my older brother came home from Harvard for Thanksgiving, I was immensely excited. I hurried home from the big boulevard that afternoon and came bounding upstairs to shake his hand, proud to be able to greet him with genuine masculine warmth and brotherly affection. "Sandy, Sandy, welcome home, goddamnittohell, you look JUST GREAT, you sonofabitchbastardyou, you're a sight for sore EYES, no kidding, it's great to have you back, youfartingsonofapisseroo, what's new, oldprick, with YOU, pal, don't pissandslipinapailofshit, man, just put'er there, boy, and shake it, kiddo, SHAKE it till it shakes your goddamn ass off or so help me, Sandy, I'll tittyshittyshoveitu pyoursstickyprickyluckyfuckysnottyclotty-cocksuckingbirdtu rdthridclasswhackoffjackoffjerkofffuckoffsuckoffasshole, you mother-fuckingfuckyou."

He was impressed. After I'd finished, he regarded me thoughtfully, cool gray eyes tightening, nostrils flaring, deliberating for one instant before he threw a swift punch at my jaw.

I've never been so surprised in my life. I was sixteen-and-a-half and he was twenty-ne, and I believe this is the only time we ever tangled physically (that is, fighting) as brothers normally do in the course of growing up. His fist only grazed my chin because I was already moving like a reflex with the punch. I caught his wrist. I jerked it forward in the direction it was coming. He followed it across the room, caromed off a chest of drawers, and bruised himself on a magazine rack.

"God *damn* you, Milly," he yelled, fetching up on the base of a floor lamp.

"Up yours, kid," I said.

"I'm sorry. I meant Willy."

"Then say so."

I could see he meant it, so I forgave him at once. I helped him up, straightening out his sweater, repressing with all my might a feeling of love, experiencing an uncomfortable desire to touch him gently on the cheek and ask him if he'd got hurt. I wondered of course what *he* felt about *me*. (But it was not the kind of thing we could discuss any more.) It wasn't entirely clear to me either why he'd been such a poor sport about my greeting, or why he'd tried to hit me. But I wouldn't ask; it was more manly not to.

He recovered his sense of humor with his breath. "New skills, Willy. Where've you been practicing *that*?"

"Oh that? Tongue-twisters, you see, if you practice tongue-twisters…"

"No, *that*."

"Oh. Haidu. School of Judo."

"Pretty fancy," he said, rubbing his cheekbone.

"Shit, that's nothing."

We shook hands warmly; he winced. (My fingers, wrists, and forearms had been getting a workout in judo exercises, three times a week in class, daily at home.) Zipped into my black leather jacket and moving with my well-oiled, muted glide, I slipped into the living room and leaned against the bookshelves on one elbow, one thumb pulling at one pocket, and looked my brother over solemnly.

He said, "Hey, what's with the new jacket?"

"Cut wrong for the Ivey League?" I asked with cool sarcasm, appraising him. He looked so dignified it was almost funny. The pointed chin and cheeks—long cheeks—and sharp fuzzless ears were what did it. His changeless gray eyes, I discovered, did change. They varied during the course of that evening from frostpane remoteness to unexpected slow thaws of tenderness. And there, etched alongside his eyes, were tiny lines that moved as if he'd just seen something funny but wouldn't say what. I *liked* him, I decided, and from my new vantage point as a boy, maybe we could be friends.

During Thanksgiving dinner, my knee kept bouncing—another method I had devised to stimulate myself. I suppose it was the excitement of having Sandy around again, or maybe only a sensation of rivalry or jealousy. Anyhow, my leg wouldn't stop, I kept thinking I was about to produce the desired result at last, and as a result, I nearly missed the big announcement.

Sandy announced (standing up to do so) a new career for himself. Medicine. He began to "dissect" the turkey. Sandy a doctor? I thought he was joking. He'd been studying physics all along hadn't he? Father disapproved of the change, too. It was late now for Sandy to change, he said. Except in physics, Sandy would be unable to get a fellowship for graduate work, and it certainly wasn't possible for Father to put Sandy through medical school. He was still paying my hospital and surgical expenses. (Hermaphroditism, I might note in passing, Is a possibility too little considered by Blue Cross. Father, we later learned, remained in debt for years while wrangling in a legal suit to crush allegations of cosmetic surgery.)

After dinner who had to wash the dishes? As always, me. Mother cleared, I washed, Sandy dried, Father phoned. To make me feel better, pretty soon Sandy wrapped a big dishtowel around his waist, shoved me aside, and continued with the dishwashing. So I just dried.

Father went out to play poker. Mother lay down for a nap.

I beckoned. I took Sandy into Father's study and went rummaging in the bottom drawer of the big desk. I asked Sandy if he wanted a glass of the stuff. He said, "Listen, put it back. I'll buy you some."

"Don't get me wrong, only a taste for me, that's all I ever take," I explained, "whenever he goes out for poker. I've got to get use to it somehow."

He made me put it back. We settled down in his old bedroom. I almost never went in there anymore. I slung my feet up across one corner of his old desk, crossing my ankles.

"Willy, what's going on with you? You're trying too hard."

"I've got to catch up."

"You've got to relax."

I shook my head. "I've got to try harder."

"You've got to *stop* trying."

"Advice is cheap. Listen, Sandy," I said, unslinging my ankles and leaning forward quickly. I pointed a slender finger at him. "I don't know a single other person in this country who's got problems like mine."

I could see that this touched him, even though that was all I said. He got up and walked around the room, then went to the window and looked out. That was all he did but it was dark, there was nothing to see, and he stayed there looking out a long time, so I knew he remembered–and still felt some of the power of the old days. I wondered if I could tell him what was giving me my newest nightmares. If I couldn't be open and honest with Sandy, of all people, with whom… so…

I told him. He pulled his head in from the window, shocked. "The doctors say the trouble spot isn't behind my fly, it's up behind the eyes. So what I want to know is just one thing. What happens inside a guy's head? What turns his switch ON and makes it go up, up, up?"

"That's a hell of a thing to ask me."

"I *have* to ask."

"I don't believe it. You already know."

"What d'you mean, I know? You mean all that malarkey the doctors hand out about desire, instinct, intercourse, sphincters? I *know* all that–but what makes it work? That I don't know. What makes it really go? What makes it go, Go, GO!"

He stared at me. Remote.

"All right," I said, "be superior."

"I'm not being superior. That's not fair."

Was he embarrassed, then? He was acting very strangely. The wings of his nose were pulsing. I inquired, "What made it go for us?" I corrected myself: "For you."

He smiled and hummed abruptly, this absurd casual stance of his only revealing his embarrassment.

I said, "Don't be a jackass, please, we *can talk* about this."

"A bull session? Go on."

His laugh wrinkles made his eyes almost wink. Was I wrong? Had I been dead wrong? Was he actually not embarrassed, but rather enjoying our "bull session"? Or embarrassed *because* he was enjoying it? As for myself, I knew I was enjoying it, partly because talking about it created a sense of freedom–freedom from it–and yet continued our sense of intimacy. "Okay, but please stop hemming and humming with me. Older brothers are *supposed* to tell their kid brothers things like this. So where does this crazy excitement, this instinct-and-desire business start from?"

Amused? Yes, he was. Was I so funny? Why? Lying down on his bed, arms behind his head, he began to preach, "Willy, it's love–"

"That makes the world go round?" I suggested. "Please don't be soupy with me," I warned him. "I've heard enough of this vague love crap already."

"Not even out of high school yet"–he clucked–"and that's not sophisticated enough?" Obligingly, he changed his tune, "Well, then, it's hate. It's hate that makes the world go round. It's love that makes it square."

I hadn't any idea whether he was being on the level with me. But I doubted it. "Sandy," I tried, "I hate-love Mom and I hate-love Pop and I can't get it up hard for either one of them."

He must have been deeply offended at this way of talking. "Milly, you're talking nonsense."

I burned red, then paled to white. I told him, "I know a jiujitsu pressure point that will paralyze half your body."

"Sorry, Willy. Relax." He closed his eyes.

"Okay. But *tell me!*" What makes it go up?"

He opened his eyes. He got off his bed, slumped down in his chair, closed his eyes. And finally he answered me with one blunt word.

I thought I was going to have a fit, a tantrum, an exhausted hysterical blow-out that would rock the room. I held on carefully and said in a low, reasonable mutter, "Are you telling me that an opening is *exciting?*" All I could think of was where and how I used to pee. It was futile to hope I could ever get excited about that, of all the god-damn-things. "Are you going to sit there and tell me that everyone alive in the country today got procreated because labia are exciting?"

"What? You're not serious… Everyone in the country…" His ears began to move by themselves, involuntarily trembling; this talk was evidently a strain for him. Yet the hidden tension in the center showed only at the edges, the sides and corners. "As you say, there's procreation, there's evolution, it's all those things, and love, and instinct, and secondary sex characteristics."

I took a long breath. "What?"

"Lots of things about a woman–her pretty face, a pair of legs, even pretty clothing–but the central thing is–" He didn't repeat it.

I thought of the raised skirt, the daily thighs. "But that's for kids isn't it?"

He shook his head.

The whole thing struck me as preposterous. I simply didn't believe Sandy's theory. There had to be more to the mystery of procreation and instinct.

A little after Thanksgiving, all my persistent hanging-around in the candy store paid off. I managed to get in with a gang of kids who used to meet at night for a little "homework," as they called it. I was invited along on extended peeping tomcat expeditions, skulking about for hours on the rooftops, scouting houses for the most promising lights. I liked the rooftop work–the silent climbing, jumping, swinging, and running–it used to remind me of games of Follow-the-Leader with Sandy. But the ultimate reward always bored me.

"J-e-e-e-sus!" whispered Whitey's unbelieving, patient voice in the darkness. "Look at the size of them."

"O-o-o-oh!" sighed the Fatman.

And buck-toothed Mickey on my left breathed, "O-h-h-h-h."

Personally, I think she knew we were out there, I wondered f Juliet knew that Romeo was out there.

"Off," pleaded Shark.

"Off," exulted Smiley softly to the night air.

We were leaning over a metal fire escape and it was shaking; you could feel the vibrations as the gang wriggled against the bars like small caged animals. As usual I felt inferior, annoyed, and a little sleepy with the dull wait. To pass the time I strained my fingers on the highest fire-escape bar, strengthening my wrists while the others were straining their eyes and their anatomy.

"Pretty little pussy. Pretty little pussy," Whitey purred.

"If you don't take 'em off–" threatened Shark.

The silence on the fire escape was black. "We gotta win," Whitey said. "We gotta. What about the girls' locker room?"

"But there ain't no windows in there, Whitey," Shark said. He put an arm consolingly around Romeo's shoulders.

"We put a hole through."

"Where to where?" said Shark, and spat down the dark alley. We padded off the fire escape like cats, and sat on the curb under a ring of light.

Was Sandy right, after all? I mulled it over. "The locker room might be easier," I said casually, I thought I saw a chance to end these interminable night waits.

"No, Shark's right, kid, forget it," Whitey said. "You got to know the layout."

"All right, so we go in and case it," I said, lighting a cigarette.

Shark was impressed but worried. "You going in there?"

"Us," I said. "In dresses. What about it? How many of you guys got the guts to go in with me?" There was a moment of cowardly thought.

"Not me," said Mickey.

"They'd spot us," said the Fatman. "We'd get in but we'd never get out."

I made a noise between my teeth to indicate my disgust. "All it takes is one kid with steady nerves," I said.

I must have been feeling pretty confident of myself by then, because the next day I showed up carrying in a parcel a dress–the same one I had worn to the gynecologist's office almost a year earlier–and a red and yellow kerchief for my head. The gang helped me get ready in the top-floor washroom. There were a few wisecracks, but on the whole everyone as tense and very serious: the stakes, they sensed, were high.

Actually my performance was almost effortless. I went in at the change of class periods, among a couple of hundred girls of various sizes and shapes. Through the commotion of zippers and sneakers, I made a seemingly casual but careful circuit of the labyrinthine locker rooms. The "layout" was far more complicated than I had imagined, and for a while I thought I would have to make an architect's drawing. But then I hit on the ingenious idea of following a flight of steps which led to the swimming pool. The place was so full of vapor from the showers, with girls milling about and towels slung all over the pipes, that it was hard to get the design of the pipes straight. I left, traced the same route in the corridor outside, went back through to the shower room to check the layout again, and then reported to Whitey.

I would have been a hero even if the plan hadn't worked. The upstairs washroom was loud with cheers. Still, I had made one staggering mistake. "But what'd ya *see?*" they pleaded with me. I had to admit I hadn't noticed much, except that the place had been full of girls. "I was busy *figuring*." Luckily, they were ready to forgive me almost anything.

That mistake, and their desperate disbelief, their impassioned will to believe that I'd observed more that floor plans, corridors, and conduits, forced me finally to believe. The female body... who in his right mind could ever have imagined... Reluctantly, I was forced to admit it. Doubting, I no longer dared to deny it. Still doubting, I had to accept it—with question-mark belief, so to speak. The incredible source of all that motive power of male desire? How unpleasant. How paltry. How funny—a joked that might be laughed at a single time if the mood was right—but how fundamentally uninteresting and irritating. Did I *have* to bother my head learning to master the riddle of desire if that was all it came to? Dante, I later read, speaks of love first entering through the yes. But that sex should enter through the eyes and from there pull the bodily strings and make that little naked unseen puppet rise and dance before its mistress seemed an unworthy image for poetry and a low image of life. Yet at sixteen I was forced to face the low facts of American sex life into which I'd been initiated, by my own choice, by my own doing, over these past weeks and months. Beauty–I hardly need to say it–had nothing to do with it: it was flesh for flesh's sake.

Of course it didn't escape me that perhaps this was only a stage… that these young men would grow older, become fathers of families, and so change… grow to find the motivation for sexual love in something less gross than this single unengrossing, rather plain item. But I doubted it. I looked at myself, something misgave me there, too. If I *had* to become a boy this way, and what other way was there, how would I emerge from the process? Their way? Another way?

The water pipes, as it turned out, came out through the wall of an unused janitor's closet in the basement storage area near the gym. Whitey jimmied the lock. Within three days Fatman, whose father was a plumber, had cleared the masonry though the wall over the sink. Just under the ceiling. Whitey, who had a fine hand with a steel bit, drilled the final wee opening–so that nothing fell through at all. A mere pinprick must have been visible on the other side. We covered the excavation on our side, when not in use, with a mirror surmounted by the school banner.

Triumphant shower-watching, standing on the sink, at first replaced all other sports and diversions. One at a time, backs were arched to the hole and necks stretched. But because of the position of the girls' shower room, the angle of vision never reached higher than the girls' shoulders, and usually only to the navel. They were so close that we couldn't see their faces. So all day long in corridors and classes the gang tried to memorize figures: only to discover how impossible it was to identify the same figures unclothed. Day after day the boys took down the mirror and pressed themselves to the small hole in paroxysms of hope, longing to recognize their conquests–in vain. Just on the other side of the pinpoint opening–hundreds and hundreds every day–flitted we soapy nameless bellies, red impersonal knees, breasts without owners, indifferently busy washcloths and fingers. Do you think the onlookers minded the impersonality, the lack of particularity? Do you imagine that pelvis without person, groin without a name or subject, ever palled? The boys kept at it for months, mesmerized by the flesh until they were numbed by it. One day Whitey said, 'Let's cat it again, what d'you say?" And that night we all took to the roofs again: "For a little excitement," Shark admitted to me with relief. Out of boredom… but it was only for more of the same, I discovered; only for a little exercise and a greater variety of the same blunt word.

I returned to the gynecologist, the surgeon. It wasn't bravery, it was only clarity. I had no choice. Forward, then. Begin again with the body of love, the eye of the hurricane, the tail of the comet. The song, the sweep, the star, the silences of desire had been too long postponed, might never be mine. They were shocked to hear my request. "It's too late," they chorused. But it's never too late. And it's never too soon either. "Make me over again," I announced. I requested nothing. I announced. "I don't want to lose my male organ, you understand. It's mine, God knows. But sew me up. Seal it in. Completely." They goggled, they laughed, they gagged, they drew diagrams, they offered scientific arguments, they launched personal attacks on me and on the imbecility, to say nothing of the unfeasibility, of my surgical desires. And over and over they wanted to know: "Why? Why?" I gave the simplest possible answer. And though they claimed not to believe me, though every man jack of them pretended to deny my reasoning, I'm sure they understood me when I told them bluntly, "Cunt."

Prelude to a Glorious Fugue

I have short hair and under my strong brows, two honest Indian-bead eyes. My face is subtle, fretful, and quick. But my flesh is weak and my spirit uncertain and by now the legend written across my smile must evidently be "Tread on me." The awful part of it is, I noticed even before he asked me how to get to thirty-fourth street that he was definitely not a type you go out with. He had the face of a star. Long pink lips with an extra bend or two. And a chin like the pry end of a hammer. "One gets so turned about in your subways," he creaked melodiously. And milky eyes. An oven door opened, hot air gusted, *Vogue* began to blow, perfect hungry women were running across my lap and leaping the stiles of my knees. I'd lost my place. He crooned with a queer accent something: "Are you native here in New York?" Or it might have been: "Do you hate it here in New York?" The lights went out. God, what did one say? "You're visiting the United States?" I am terribly highpitched, and witless in the dark. The lights went on. I was staring at his eyebrows. In them, sweat like misplaced tears.

I feast on Sunday, fast on Monday, perspire on Tuesday,

desire all Wednesday, despair by Thursday, and prepare each Friday (hidden in the agency library where I consume iced coffee all day long) miracles of medical advertising copy– "pre-TENSE eliminates the past TENSE in TENSion. And leaves attention unimpaired." Layout–photo cut of bewildered young woman; suggest ink drawing of ganglion across her face.

So I gave him my phone number. I am low-bred, open-hearted, and partial to foreigners.

And in the middle of all that heat, Saturday, he phoned. I was showering. I took his name, by now forgotton, from dictation. Ferenci? English? I stared at the wet pad after I hung up. He worked for the BBC in London, he said. So stupidly, on account of his Brittish hornpipe or whatever the tune that served his voice, I overdressed. I dressed to meet a spy. It was after 5 when I got to the Statler. Over the noisy house phone he said, "Won't you come up? I'm washing the jelly."

"What?"

"I said come up. Drinks are here."

But when I opened the door he was not the man I'd met. I refused to enter the room-rooms, a suite, people, noise, a party in full gallop. Near the door of the salon, watching TV, sat this most unpleasantly handsome type. Ferenci without a doubt-I did and did not recognize him.

He had pocky, sweaty, luminous flesh. His eyes worked independantly of his mouth, his oval eyes and wiggly mouth were thinking separate thoughts. His lower lip had tiny unshaven fish barbels bristling beneath it. How could it be that he was still attractive for all this, it's impossible to say.

But he was, in a razor like way that made my skin back up. He leaned from the TV set-towards me in the doorway-with a spine more flexible than I had ever seen, swaying slightly, awash with currents. He wore a T-shirt (a T-shirt!) over an assertive chest and when he spoke, his periscoping mouth unshuttered, galactic with teeth. "Tell us who you are," he said to me. "Even myself, I hardly know you." Looking back, I wonder if I could have guessed that they were putting me through a test.

The dark girl sitting across the room on the sofa said with the sudden amazing force of a practiced elocutionist, making her nostrils flare, "Darling, give me a ciggarette." To me?

"Do close the door." Ferenci more friendly.

"What's your first name?" I logically demanded.

Not immediately, he turned off the set. "Maurice." It was almost Morris. "Why?" he said.

"And Ferenci? You're Italian?"

"Does it matter? Come in now, do, dear. I'm one tablespoon English, two teaspoons Italian, and a teaspoon Ferenczy," he gargled. "Father was Hungarian, but he changed the spelling when he came to Italy. That's where he met mother. Dear, do come in."

I did. And sat. In a straight chair. A man motionless on the sofa exclaimed, "I'm *Kenneth!*" he had damp flesh. His features were pulled wide apart like a stretched sweater, and at once I distrusted him. He inquired solicitously, "Do you like it here at the Statler?"

I said, astonished, "Yes." For no reason.

"Good!" And out of the back room noisy with dance music, someone with lustrous pants and a purple shirt, with swarthy skin and long curling sideburns, snaked across the carpet to meet me. In the midst of one gyration he captured a glass from the coffee table and sat. We were introduced.

"Reynold's a painter," my Ferenci explained, handing me a drink.

He was followed out of the back room by a blonde girl who chose her seat carefully, sitting first near me, then on second thought between the dark girl and Kenneth on the sofa. "Who's this girl?" Reynolds said. I thought he might mean her. She had golden down on the sides of her arms and the back of her neck, the kind that glints under light. She frowned and refocused her contact lenses. Reynold's voice lilted, "Who are you?" He came spinning at me like a trout line. "I've got to know you. I'm not going to let anyone sit here hiding her identity." Undulating, he got down on the floor next to my chair. "Let's see your legs. Let's see." And he put his head on my lap, running his hand up my ankle.

I flushed into sweat. I tried to push him off, but instead pushed chair and table. Glasses flashed. "I'm going to leave," I explained. My instincts are sound.

Soothingly, Ferenci took my hand. I didn't want him to take my hand. For one thing, my hand was wet. "Did he shock you?"

"As a matter of fact, yes." The right answer, it turned out.

Reynolds rose from the floor and swayed toward Kenneth. "Isn't that why you practice medicine?"

"Yes, medicine is a basic form of epistemology," Kenneth pronounced.

"I had to know if she was fat, didn't I?"

"It's all right now, Maurice said, elegant screen star. He

was the most preferable man in the room. I looked from that immobile face to the others, Kenneth's, the blonde girl's, the dark girl's. The blonde girl said nothing that whole time, but her orange jumper recited passionately for her. Its articulation revealed rich communications taking place on the sofa between herself and Kenneth. On the other side the two women were holding hands.

"'Nita's fat, Reynolds confided to me. The dark girl was 'Nita.

Even in this heat she was wearing a shapeless sweater. "It's not fat," she boomed to me. "It's his baby I'm carrying in there." Her jaw clearly indicated Kenneth. For reasons now known to me, she told me this venomously, a warning rattle in her throat.

Ferenci said quietly, his lips to his glass, "Keep your eyes on Kenneth. He's famous for being able to make a girl achieve her climax while sitting a foot away from her."

I clenched my fingernails into my palms–not to move–I wouldn't have moved now if Maurice Ferenci and all the other chiller-killer spies who acted for the BBC in London had been pulling hairs out of my head.

The blonde girl set fire to the cigarette pack in the ashtray, she gave me a meaningful look, signifying, I believe, nothing, the cellophane began turning brown, and Kenneth spoke expansively, "Reynold, listen. Maurice's new girl's wonderful." He grew lyrical, rapturous. He filled the air with conviction. "She's a *wonderful* girl!" He smiled at me. I smiled back. How had it suddenly turned out that Kenneth was on my side?

I let them bundle me into the cab, Maurice and Kenneth, I don't know why—unfed in all that dying heat, I suppose.

Convinced that dinner was my due. Dr. Kenneth Garrison had invited us to come eat with him—we were on a last name basis at last—and my spy dress was soon affixed with rubber cement to the leatherette seat. I still have no idea what happened to the rest of them.

"So you met her on the subway," Dr. Garrison mused out loud. I managed to keep more than a foot away from him, thirteen inches between us, hard as this is when you are sticking to the rear seat of a cab beween two men. The meter clicked on—east, across town. Dr. Garrison, I had understood, lived on the west side, uptown. I was being abducted by a Dr. Kenneth Garrison, a Maurice Ferrenci, and the cabdriver? I memorized his face, name, and number on the photo.

Maurice's speaking, silent-screen eyes looked me over. His eyes said, Ah-there-are-untapped-reservoirs-within-you. He said this twice before speaking. Then he added, "You're not *really* American?"

"I'm typical U.S.A.," I annunced. I had finished college. I was making money. I was on a diet.

From his corner, Dr. Kenneth said, "You've been married once, haven't you?"

Had he said that? The truck noise was ferocious—did marriage show up medically in the bloodshot corners of the eyes seven years later? And because his diagnostic stare was on my legs, I crossed them. They are slim. Beneath the knees. I didn't answer. Turning to the first person I ever allowed to succeed in picking me up on the subway, I saw a spot of perspiration spreading on the chest of Ferenci's T-shirt.

We got out at Madison Avenue. They took me to a

hamburger joint. I hadn't the presence of mind to object. It was the smallest surprise of the evening but it left me stunned.

Humburgers arrived. I ordered iced coffee. There was only hot coffee. I insisted on iced coffee. The red erupted crust of the dying earth could billow away for all I cared into roaring gases if I didn't get iced coffee tonight. The obliging waitress brought me a lump of ice in a spoon. My cup spilled over.

Maurice Ferenci cut his hamberger into six parts before eating it. I'm not sure I can expain why, but this made it difficult for me to swallow my own. I sat watching the two of them eat. The Hungarian-Italian-British one said, "She's a medical copywriter, Kenneth, ask her a question." Chewing pause. "A medical question."

I didn't recall discussing my job, this evening or on the subway. I had, however, other recollections. I said, "I was invited to dinner at the home of a friend of yours. A Dr. Kenneth Garrison I believe."

The friend tightened his lips, so I knew he was going to speak. "Oh?" he said. And he called out loud to the busy waitress running across the room, "My wife Anita is pregnant. Can you bring the relish?"

The first person finished the fifth sixth, and then explained, "You see, the evening simply had to be changed. Kenneh here has two children and always when his wife is pregnant, as I'm sure he'll be the first to admit, he feels this beastly urge. This horribly strong urge to go out with other girls."

Dr. Garrison sipped. Coffee spilled from his chin. His neck was unshaved. He remarked, "Does she have any friends, Maurice?"

I said promptly, "None at all."

Maurice stared at me with his egg-white long-lashed eyes blinking slowly. "When I rang her up this afternoon she assured me" (I was the third person) "that here in America I was expected to come pick her up at *her* place. Is that quite, how shall I say, Kenneth–is that *usual* in your country?"

"It's guaranteed in the Constitution," I opined.

Finishing his sixth sixth, he looped, dropped his napkin into his waterglass, sopped, mopped his fingertips. "Is there perhaps some superstition here, perhaps to do with meeting a man in his hotel rooms?"

The waitress removed my uneaten hamburger.

Dr. Garrison leaned and inquired darkly, "What do *hotel rooms* mean to you?" With deep psychoanalytic mien he urged, "What do the words *hotel rooms* bring up to your mind?"

"Apple pie and ice cream," I said. Garrison stared.

"Vanilla?"

"Please."

"We're fresh out of vanilla," the waitress said.

My heart broke. I sighed heavily.

Maurice patted my hand paternally and asked, "What's the most unhappy you've ever been in your life?"

I sipped diluted cofee, second cup, and answered,

"Haven't you been married once already?"

"Of course," he replied, "for six years. I've got a little sparrow of a daughter over in Milan, with her mother. I visit once a year."

The slithery arc of his smile, the pitching and rolling of that voice, was politely British. But there was a bass, leathery strain like cargo in the hold, invisibly swaying. I touched my tongue to the ice in the bottom of my cup and my thoughts were on long marriage–my thirty-two months and twenty-five days–almost three years of tearstained tablecloths and pillowcases, blouses and handkerchiefs, sheets and kleenex–a white sale of total recall.

They let me struggle out of the door first. But they guarded me one on each side. They crossed Madison Avenue with me, the three of us unswerving over its lava tar, the planet's ash still warm in our nostrils. We walked only a block to one of those splendid but badly lighted lobbies off Fifth Avenue where every door inside is labelled RING AND ENTER DR this, that, or another. One read DR. KENNETH GARRISON, but he stopped–key in hand–at an unmarked side door. He intoned, "Do you mind if Maurice comes with me?" I didn't mind. I wasn't lying. I rang and entered his waiting room and waited. One patient, just one to go. What doctor saw patients on Saturday night?

The woman sat reading VIVA. No wedding band, veiny ankles sticking out of polka dots. Hat and veil. She said, "Are you from out of town, too?"

"No."

"Most of Dr. Garrison's patients, I come to him once a week, it's without fail if you ask, they're from this or that state. Don't you think he's grand?"

"He's famous," I said.

A pigeonlike stare out of one eye. I bored the lady to VIVA. After a minute, "I'm not sick," she said, "it's a discomfort they don't know what to do with, believe me, I'm from Idaho, I've tried the lot of them."

But from the inner door out came Dr. Garrison in a

medical gown. The idaho lady puckered to attention. He bent over her officially and said in caressing tones, "As for you, my dear, you've been a delinquent patient, haven't you?"

"My vacation–"

"My dear, you ought to cancel–"

"But I did, I did cancel–"

"Did you. Well, you're in luck, because we have with us in the office this evening," she rose, and he took her by the hand, "a visiting specialist from England."

A queasy emptiness in my stomach like an elevtor dropping under me. He had sucked the lady from Idaho out through the door. I felt I ought to call for help, I ought to phone Bernie or Lyon or mother or leave. But I sat. Ferenci: the visiting specialist from England.

On the empty receptionists's desk in the waiting toom, the yellow phone rang softly. When it stopped, I heard the sounds of running water and voices inside . . . then coughing . . . a short scream. I got up quick and pressed my ear to the inner door very hard, so hard that my earlobe, still infected, just where I'd had to pull the earring out last week, hurt. Tittering. I heard it distinctly. Had the little scream before been a little laugh? And then abruptly. Close to my wall, in clearly fainting tones, "Oh Doctor! Oh Doctor!" the ladylike voice from Idaho, "Is this the British method?"

I took the leatherette chair farthest from that wall and picked up a magazine and started a crossword puzzle.

When Maurice finally reappeared, he came in wearing a white medical gown. "Have you been bored?" He was– yes, almost new again. I had not really remembered him. His once elongated lips were cherub-small. His little fish bristles were gone. His eyes quivered sensitively, happily, as he breathed through his mouth. English promises. "We'll be going downtown presently. Kenneth'll be along. Hold on tight. Gear little palace he's got on to. Like to cast an eye around? Make a splendid set, now wouldn't it just?"

And so on. I saw nothing but gear, and nothing splendid–a tour of the inner office rooms, Maurice bouncing alongside as if he had sneakers on. He kept pushing the flat of his hand to the small of my back. Three or four drab air conditioned rooms. Every air conditioner made unpleasant noises– different ones–scales, cabinets, examining tables, flouroscope, sterilizers–I stood on the second scale I saw and I slid the weights across the bars. "Go away–over *there*," I squeaked. "The other side of the room. I want to check my bathroom scale at home. Stop that."

He said, "I want to check up on *this* scale," weighing my rear, "an old-fashioned method is best."

It is very hard for me to give up a man, harder than you will believe. Visiting specialist? "Do I or don't I remember your telling me you worked for the BBC in London?"

"Dear, do I or don't I remember there's a little question of *mine*?"

What question. Something about unhapiness. "Are you an actor?" I insisted.

"God no! Exchange programs between the BBC and your American channels. That's why I'm here, you see?"

"You said you were here on vacation."

His good humor vanished. "Now that will do, dear, I dislike to be harried and pounced on before I'm actually married."

Had he said that? My shoulders snapped back so fast they hurt. I said, "Would you please turn off that *air conditioner*?"

He stared. His cheerfulness returned. "Of course. Why?" He made no move.

"Because I want to hear what you're saying and it's louder than you are. You're a medical specialist from England, according to Dr. Garrison?" A few facts were in order.

He snickered unexpectedly. "Oh that. No of course not, that was Kenneth's sick little joke. Are you annoyed? Kenneth has rather an original sense of comedy. He had me floating about in there with her, wearing this doctor's smock and sporting a stethoscope." He took off the medical gown. Down to his T-shirt again. "Then he suggests out loud I take his patient's blood pressure. I was caught a bit off guard, you know."

Was it a sick joke only? It was a bad dream. Maurice was almost giggling—a staccato leap up from his Adam's apple, a plucked string. "Do you realize," I unashamedly moralized, "that for letting you practice medicine without a license, he can be sued for malpractice?"

"Listen, do you know how to turn this off?" The air conditioner. He pinched and pulled at a knob, gave up, and returned back to me, his mouth an inch from mine so I thought he was going to kiss me, and said, "This entire marvelous office quack-quack-quack," he tootled like a duck. "Didn't you guess? Malpractice, my dear, is hardly the word for it!"

"He's a faith-healer?"

"Nothing so useful. He rents this office at mountainous sums from an acquaintance, some young intern or resident who's a genuine physician, or so I hear. Kenneth's tastes are somewhat specialized, and since fortunately he has his wife Anita's inheritance now, you see . . ." again the plucked guitar snicker, "this friend of his is taking some sort of postdoctoral degree in psychiatry on *Kenneth's* money, and Ken has simply taken over his office. Not his practice. Kenneth's patients are actually his own, they get sent to him from hotels, ladies all, he kicks back part of the fee to the hotel desk clerks, and the most unbelieveable part in all this is, you know dear, *they do keep coming back* to him, the ladies do."

The nearest chair on the other side of Maurice was too far away, and besides, it had by now become a test of endurance. "You are telling me that Kenneth in there isn't a doctor?"

Saliva flashed on his cheery lips. "His Doctor, that's authentic. But not in medicine. Kenneth's a Ph.D. In psychology—he does analysis with patients at a clinic. He's just started. That's how he met this what's-his-name doctor, he won't reveal the name."

I had to sit. I sidled past. He patted me again as I moved but that was the least of it—physician, psychiatrist, psychologist. "He'll be arrested. Both of them."

"I doubt it. This doctor who sublets to Kenneth isn't legally required to check on Kenneth's license, one couldn't expect that, and Ken's bloody careful about things like prescriptions, he writes only—damn it!—prescriptions for mineral salts and fishfoods. Ssssss!"

The "damn it!" seemed to have stopped the machine, it sighed to silence. Maurice's reptile warning must have meant "Shhhhh!" because he slipped immediately to a closed door I hadn't noticed and flattened himself to it in a fluid movement that was not without grace. Like me? I have never seen anyone so two-dimentional, so flat against a door. More expert than me. Oppressed, I saw his knack for making me feel in cahoots with him.

He whispered, barely moving his lips, "He's still in there with her!"

The truth, maybe the lady had come for a fix, heroin from Idaho? I am skeptical. I sat. I stood. I said deliberately, loud, "But why? I mean—to be crude about it—what's in it for him? He's a psychologist. The professional and legal risks, they're enormous."

He came away from the door and spoke softly, indulgently, "Kenneth says he's a frustrated physician at heart. But between me and you, dear, he enjoys giving people a mild hurt now and again. He never does them serious harm. It's not easy, you know, to find willing victims, and it's hard for him to live without. That's why he's becoming an analyst."

I tried my best. "Is that the British method, Doctor?"

I'd admitted eaversdropping. He didn't care. He confessed, too. "Oh Doctor! Oh Doctor! Lord, she was terrible. That was when I put that elastic blood-pressure thing round her thigh. Believe me, it was a relief for both of us. Because first, wouldn't you know, I'd wound that rubber apparatus so tight round the old bird's arm, she turned green when I inflated it and started whistling through her teeth. I couldn't get the damn thing off her arm, I had it so twisted. There's a button you press, this I find out later, but Kenneth don't even show by a sign, and all this while the old girl's huffing away in a ghastly pathetic fright."

Weep or shrug? Be sick or be calm? My logic was

impeccable. "I'm afraid either I don't understand you," I said, "or else I'm afraid I do."

He gave me a slow gentlemanly smile and squint—sign language—with a sliding back of the head that meant come here. I didn't. He said, "How about you?"

I concluded, "I don't understand."

He stroked the spot beneath his luxurious lower lip reflectively, apparently concentratiing on the problem he had about shaving himself there. "With your husband, let me ask you, did you ever enjoy reaching that climax they talk about?"

I answered not one word.

"Men have that trouble, too," he said.

I searched his mushroom chin, his nightshade cheeks, for traces of humor. None.

"I am that way–"he confided, "like you—the other way." I'd heard every word, the air conditoner was off, there could be no mistake. He said, "I know more than you imagine— about you—that first moment on the subway, I don't know how I knew, but it's in your face, it's in that voice you have, I hear it, it's like hearing music."

"What music?"

"A prelude."

He said that. I paused, a thoughtful two-measure rest. "It may not matter to you at all that I don't want to have anything further to do with you."

"No, it doesn't matter," he said. "I knew perfectly, I didn't need to be told how much and how little anxious you were to see me this evening. That's percisely why I rang you up. When I can think of anything else you'll detest, I'll ask you to do that, too."

I am not entirely without insight. This imported man, I guessed what power he had over me. The power of my own revulsion. "Is that why you brought me *here*?"

He replied indirectly. "Why not do this," he suggested, "why not cancel all your plans for tomorrow, Sunday, come to my hotel room all the day, you'll have a glorious time."

"No."

"At eleven in the morning."

Nor am I normally weak in the shins.

"It will be disagreeable for you," he said, "very disagreeable, you'll have to ask for my room number, for you see, I won't tell you it again now, and the desk clerk will give you a knowing stare, my room at eleven in the morning or even at ten, and upstairs the women maids on my floor will all stand there, looking you over, watching you as you go hunting down the hall, looking for my room number." While speaking he lit a cigarette. He lay down on the examining table stretched out–smoking, flat, absorbed in his prediction. "There are some women, you know, who can't enjoy themselves unless–" the smoke over his face flickered. "It seems a pity not to try to find out."

I thought I'd missed a sentence. "Find out what?"

"There's so little time. I'm going back to London."

"I've been propositioned before," I said. "This one comes with a time limit."

Coldblooded, he inquired, "With your husband, did it ever really hurt?"

I saw him now, a polished statue that had been left out of doors for centuries and had got chipped in the genitals. He was saying, "The number of things two people can do together is limited. But the frightfulness in it for both of them can be pretty much without limit." That much I knew. It had been coming at me from a long way, from childhood or farther back, from history and fairytales, from a thousand and one nights.

"I hope you'll all be arrested tomorrow," I keened. In my sorrow I hoped that even the lady from Idaho would be convicted. And me too.

The Search

The arrival in Paris of his dead wife's sister brought him a new, unwanted hate. In his bedroom she was an alien presence. She seemed to smell of some irritating, oddly indelicate perfume, as though, he thought, she had carefully applied it to obscure whatever gentler, more feminine odors were secreted in the recesses of her body. The confined chamber of air, pressed down by the sloping eaves, had held till now only familiar odors: the animal smell of pajamas, the smell of sheets and pillows which reminded him sometimes of the sea, and the stale paperlike smell of cheap furniture. The eaves themselves, sweating a coat of moisture, seemed to add to this system of odors. A new scent had disturbed the arrangement. Pearce rolled over in bed.

The bedroom was perpetually cold. The stove managed to heat only the kitchen in which it stood. In the bedroom, water condensed on the cold plaster eaves. On the kitchen stove, a pot of boiling water gave up incessant vapor to the ceiling.

For two days before his dead wife's sister had arrived in Paris, Pearce had been running a fever. He met her at the train anyhow, a little unsteady on his feet. Clouds of steam gushed from the train's belly, the crowds struggled by him on each side. When he recognized her, as she stepped from the train onto the quai, when she flicked her hips around, and he saw her face, partly foreign yet intimately known, his burden of hate settled upon her. Inexorably, the family resemblance had marked her features. His accumulated hatred found, in this strong resemblance, sufficient excuse, sufficient outlet. Its weight, shifting suddenly to a faintly-known sister, caught Pearce off-balance, but willing. Their meeting was brief.

Sydney spend three days in Paris. On the fourth, she contrived to get Pearce to leave with her on a hasty trip into Brittany. She spent her days in Paris pursuing a round of enquiries into the circumstances of her sister's death. But Paris was cold, was in fact extraordinarily bitter, and people were tight-mouthed and in a hurry. From Pearce she could get little. He knew only the barest details—these she investigated—and moreover he was ill. She nursed him in her spare time. His apartment was small, unpleasant, but better than the utter isolation of her hotel room. The long line of his body, swelling the quilt hour by hour in a succession of shifting ridges, showed her a man struck down and made passive by tragedy. The spectacle was repugnant, it aroused in her contempt, but the very tension of that contempt made his sickroom more bearable than the blank squares of other rooms.

"Tea is ready," she called in to him, lifting the pot from the stove. She prepared the tea. In the bedroom, a few moments later, they drank it. Pearce sat up to drink, a heavy dark coat thrown around his shoulders.

"I've talked to some of Pierre's friends," she said.

"Friends?"

"They know him. Not well. Can't you tell me anything more about him?"

Pearce gulped the hot tea down his gullet. He could feel it enter his stomach, it was so hot. He repeated again, in the same words he had always used to Sydney: "He is a member of The Friends of Krishna. He rides a motorcycle."

Sydney got up, exasperated, and went to the window, where she stood sideways, looking out and drinking her tea.

Her presence in the room annoyed Pearce. The angular outline of her body, in clothes that were tailored with a flair, angered him. The ruff at her chest and throat, the flare of her jacket over her hips, the neat fall of the grey skirt down her legs, all were too clean and too precise for the shadow life that absorbed his days. Their lines, their stuffs, their stitching and pattern overrunning her body called to him and threatened to reawaken him,

"You're not sick," she said suddenly, turning upon him in anger.

Pearce smiled. "I have a hundred point five."

"You're in bed, horribly in bed. Get out of bed. Your fever will go away anyhow."

"Listen," she continued, coming closer and sitting on the edge of his bed, "never mind that. Probably you'd do better in bed. But I know where Pierre is." She paused to allow the effect of her words to reach Pearce. "I know where he lives. That is, I know where his parents live, and I know he is with them now. He may be staying there only another few days. After that nobody has any idea where to find him. Is your car available? Can you drive it in your condition?"

"Where do they live?"

"In Brittany, near Carhaix."

"Where?"

"Near Carhaix." She watched him closely. She had lied. She had learned the address of Pierre's parents, but she had no notion whatever whether Pierre himself was there now. And it would be incautious to telephone. The image of her sister flickered tentatively in her mind, but would not realize itself, would not make itself visible. Nevertheless, Pearce *should* go, she would see that he went, sick or healthy, to confront Pierre. "Well?" she queried.

"We'll leave tomorrow."

She had won. She had struck upon the one demand which could still be made on Pearce's existence.

They left Paris the next morning. At about four o'clock Pearce's fever began to bother him, but he drove on till almost six.

At the very start, in the morning, they had had some difficulty finding their way out of Paris. Following the wide boulevards that border the outlying sections of the city, they managed at last, despite a few false turns, to leave behind the sheltering tenement houses lining their route, and the scurrying interfering traffic. They issued slowly into freer country. They skirted the palace at Versailles. The land flattened out. Even the hills were flatter than the heaving tenements, now behind, that reared their glassy eyes to the sun. There were few cars now. Pearce felt liberated. He eased into the seat.

As their distance from Paris drew itself longer and longer, Pearce made an effort to reflect on the purpose of their trip–on *his* purpose, at all events. But his thoughts would not obey his desire. They carried him to the point where he recognized that he must see Pierre, but beyond that they would not march. He felt only a cramping resentment of his sister-in-law, intolerable that she should be sitting beside him! His resentment fixed itself, in fact, on her clothes, which she had specially chosen for that day for car travel, and which in their unrelieved and simple tailored style, seemed to Pearce harsh, inhuman. He could not get his mind away from the conviction that she was unsexed and therefore to be feared. At the bottom of a long hill along which the road seemed to stretch and unfurl itself above their heads like an overhanging cliff, he realized that his motives in this trip were not his own, that they belonged to the woman beside him, and he had a sudden uneasy inkling of where they might end. Up ahead on the road, a black dot silhouetted against the sky at the summit of the hill grew to the tiny figure of a man. Pearce wondered who stood there against the mottled sky, and glanced quickly at Sydney. His muscles tightened against the wheel and accelerator, as though he were restraining himself from striking a blow; the car shot more quickly ahead, and it was as if some enemy thought, offspring of the unsexed, unwomanly woman at his side, had stabbed him. His mind had become such a teeming cage of images he could not bear to face, that it was a relief to see the spot at the top of the hill take shape as a policeman whose hand was raised in a command: "Stop!" Pearce slowed down. He stopped.

The officer approached the car from Sydney's side and poked his helmeted head in at the window, asking Pearce what he thought he was doing driving up the middle of the road, and demanding to see his driver's license and *carte grise.*

With a start Pearce realized that he had been driving up the entire hill in the center lane of a three-lane highway. He handed over his papers and said, "We're foreigners."

The officer said nothing, took the papers, and stepped away from the car to read them. Sydney got out and began to converse with the patrolman. Pearce watched the smooth line of her back momentarily, but his eye was caught by the police motorcycle waiting at the side of the road, a black compact mass of details: cylinders, springs, wires, wheels, tanks. The door opened and Sydney got back in. The officer returned Pearce's papers and said, "The center lane is used only to pass other cars. Be careful. Otherwise you risk heavy penalties." He glanced admiringly at Sydney. "All right," he concluded, "go on. Goodbye."

Pearce started the car. He asked no questions, annoyed that he owed to Sydney the avoidance of a fine; to the fact, moreover, that someone had apparently found her attractive.

They stopped for a bite to eat in the early afternoon, and then continued westward. When Pearce's fever returned perceptibly to his body, he decided that it did not interfere with his driving, and he kept on, though more and more slowly. As night fell and Pearce's head grew painfully dizzy with the effort of concentration, they stopped in a small town, at the sign of a hotel. But only one room was available. At the second hotel, the only other in town, an incident occurred which scattered the prearranged pattern of their emotions.

They found the hotel with some difficultly on a side street and entered the door at which the sign hung, only to find a small, unpopulated café. Sydney, in apprehension, drew back as a large fat man entered suddenly from behind a curtain they had not seen. Yes, he said, they did have a room, yes, two rooms, but the hotel was located a few minutes from here. Another fat man entered. They whispered together briefly, and the first fat man said that "the car was ready." The soiled dinginess of the café had put Sydney's back up. In part her misgiving communicated itself to Pearce; in part an inner qualm of his own exerted its force against his tired passivity. He said, "Can we see the rooms first?"

"Yes," said the fat man, "I'll take you in my car."

"But we can drive ourselves."

"Ah no, it is not far. I am going to take you."

Pearce's weariness yielded. The fat man's car was like a hearse, black, with a large empty compartment in the rear. Sydney shifted her knees from side to side, anxiously, and asked the driver his occupation. He was, he said, owner of the hotel and the café. The car raced downhill at a frightening speed through dark, narrow streets no wider than itself.

The hotel, only four short blocks away, was reached in a matter of seconds. They entered first a totally black court, bewildering in its unexpected opaqueness, and passed along a brief black alley, through a wooden door, and up two flights of rotten wooden staircase. The hotel had obviously not been used for a long time. The unrelieved darkness disturbed the edges of Sydney's thinking. Discipline put her through the required motions easily, but she wanted to run.

The keys the fat man had brought apparently did not work. They descended, and he indicated a dim room. "Wait in there for me," he said. "I'll find the right keys."

Pearce and Sydney looked in at a large, badly-lighted, greying plaster walls. They went inside hesitantly. Behind them, the fat man slammed the door, and in answer crowds of grey-white bed sheets, suspended from the ceiling like thoughts of affliction, shivered in the breeze.

Sydney's eyes swung around. Her mind jumped forward and she realized, in an odd surge of anticipation, that she was about to become afraid. As the fat man's footsteps receded down the passage, she tried the door, and it refused to open. She was seized at once by fear of the unaccountable, of its power to lay hold of a situation, alter its course and very shape beyond recognition, snapping from within the most balanced plans by natural and therefore irrational causes. When she could she said, "The door's locked. Let's get out the window."

Pearce examined the door. "Don't be silly, it's an automatic lock, that's all. A mistake. He'll let us out when he comes back."

But dread generated its own energy. She went to the window. It was unlocked, she saw, and at ground level. "Do you have the car keys?"

"They're in the ignition."

She thought of their isolation, their money. Nobody knew where they were. In case of trouble, she thought, they would be stronger if separate. One of them could inform the police. Perhaps the other fat man was robbing the car. "I'm going," she said. She was intensely anxious, but under control.

"How will I decide about the rooms?" Pearce asked perversely.

"Decide by yourself." She left.

Pearce waited. The inside of the coal stove gleamed redly in the corner, and he stood there, rubbing his hands dryly together over it. Sydney's fear had been somewhat contagious, but at bottom he disbelieved. The fever in his brain had already jarred reality sufficiently, and he felt this irregular course of events to coincide with his expected version of an entangled world. Yet, convinced only of confusion and not of evil intentions, he remained apprehensive. Each unforeseeable, unwanted event added to his bewilderment, reinforced his belief in unlimited possibility; and with the slowing down of his reflexes and his attendant dizziness, he was like a confused caterpillar poked and shoved by a boy's stick, by an unseen assailant.

He huddled over the stove in perplexed doubt. Disbelief was characteristic of him. He had never been able to believe fully in his wife's death. Knowing it be true, he still had never quite accepted it as irrevocable. He was, he knew, too weak to do so. He had therefore avoided, as much as possible, all but the necessary arrangements for her funeral. He had not gazed upon her in her coffin; he had not enquired into the details of the accident; he had not sought out Pierre. He had wished at all costs to avoid any final realization. And now, impelled by the ceaseless wish of her sister, he was being driven to the very castle of the enemy. Yet he felt forced to go, perhaps by the very fact of his inner disbelief. At odds with himself, therefore, wrapped in a fever, all things seemed equally disjointed, confounded. Every step seemed a mad approach to the enemy's stronghold, in a land of illogical shadows. Fearless, he wanted to run away.

While he stood there the fat man came back. He unlocked the door from the outside and came in, slamming the door. The sheets waved. "Madam has left?" he said questioningly. Pearce nodded. "Well," he confided, "I've sent my boy to get the keys. Just wait, It won't be long." The hotel owner's bulky figure, in black, ill fitting clothing, leaned over the stove too, blocking off the red glitter entirely, as though drawing it up into himself. Suddenly he said, "I have some other keys." He went into the small cupboard and withdrew a key ring. He let Pearce out, and together they remounted the stairs. But the new keys did not work. Halfway down again, they were met by a small boy of about twelve, who produced breathlessly and without a smile another ring of keys. They went upstairs again, and again the keys failed to open the door.

"Never mind," Pearce insisted over the owner's apologies. "I'm going. I don't want the room."

"Don't leave. Just one moment."

"Never mind."

"You can't leave after all this." He turned to his boy.

"I'm going."

"No, no, no, no, no, no." He whispered something in the boy's ear, and the child seemed to spring in one bound out through the hall window. "My boy will open it from inside."

Stunned by the boy's extraordinary disappearance, and obligated by the owner's requests, Pearce paused while the boy worked his way somehow around the outside of the building into the room. The door suddenly began to rattle. Inside the child cursed foully. He banged with sharp fury at the lock, and the door shook futilely. Pearce turned to go. "No!" shouted the owner. The door lurched open. In the difficult light from the small bulb at the ceiling Pearce made out a small bed, a chair, a *bidet*, a sink, and an overturned table. The soiled wallpaper curled away from the wall in great patches. It was obvious to him at once that neither he nor Sydney would have any rest or any peace of mind there. He turned to go. "I don't want to take the room."

But the owner brushed quickly past Pearce down the stairs and turned, blocking the way. "No!" he said, his face screwed up as though he were about to weep. "Stop!"

Pearce hesitated. He was confused. "I don't want to take the room," he repeated.

The owner hissed at him. "I can't permit you to leave."

"I don't understand."

"That doesn't make any difference. You must take the room. It's a question of what's right." His fat face, two steps below Pearce, looked like an ugly, angry child's.

"I don't want the room."

All at once, all the lines of the owner's face twisted up into a smile. "Please," he said, giving the words great emphasis, as though this must settle the matter, "*I, I, I want* you to take the room. It's a *good* room. I will wait on you myself." He hesitated, expecting an answer. He added, "You will have everything."

Pearce's head hurt. He didn't want the room. It seemed so simple. How ridiculous to argue. "No," he said, dully.

The lines of the owner's face suddenly contorted in new directions. He regarded Pearce with the look of one who at last recognizes a traitor. He turned to the boy who still remained passively waiting on the landing above. "Come!" he shouted venomously. Then he turned again to Pearce, deliberately spat full in his face, and clumsily descended down the stairs.

Shocked and totally unnerved, Pearce made his way downstairs wiping his face randomly with the back of his hand. When he reached the ground floor, the owner had disappeared. Pearce could hear the boy beginning to come down from the landing. He turned hurriedly out into the courtyard and groped his way through the darkness into the semi-lighted street.

He felt as if he had escaped from something terrible, and yet the night, even outside in the street, seemed to offer only momentary relief. He felt plunged and held down, as by a weight, in an unknown land, a sea bottom of half-familiar shapes and softened noises in which he and the night were not wholly distinguishable, but mingled in large, uneasy movements. When he perceived Sydney running, shakily towards him down the hill, he felt that they would collide, that their heavy, slow-moving strides were undeflectable in the liquid night.

They went back to the first hotel at which they had enquired and spent the night together in the one available room there. Pearce, whose mind did not admit of meditation, felt nevertheless hazily neutral toward Sydney. He ate a slight supper in the hotel dining room and retired at once to bed.

Sydney lingered over her meal. Her wait for Pearce at the car had been an ordeal from which she had not yet recovered. While she stood alone in the cold evening by the empty car, her brain had labored through an eternal paralyzed moment and conceived in fear the most impossible phantasms of his loss or her defeat. Now, piecing together the fragments of her will seemed an intolerable effort. Remembrance of her sister's life stung her till she almost cried, and still the picture of her sister's face refused to focus in her mind. Tenaciously she clung to her decision. Pierre *should* be brought to account. The vacuity of Pearce's existence embittered her, soured the motive of her intent. That she should be compelled to use, as an instrument for the work, a husk of manhood so vitiated and drained, was, she saw, hard. Yet the encumbrance itself sustained her, strengthened her. She pushed the untasted food from her. Her appetite, whetted by her anxious wait for Pearce, suffered itself to be denied. Appetite gave way to discipline. She would not want to eat until she had recovered, despite Pearce, despite Pierre, the full and blooded image of her sister.

Upstairs in the medium-sized room, well-appointed and brightly lighted, she prepared for bed. When she had entered and flicked on the light, she had found Pearce awake in bed, lying on his back, his wide, heated eyes turned up toward the ceiling. Occasionally they followed her movements in the room. She consulted a map, taken form her purse, and observed their position, estimated the time of their arrival tomorrow. Steeling her mind with this purpose, she nevertheless had difficulty in undressing, conscious of his open eyes upon her. When it came to her slip, she hesitated, gritting her teeth with a trace of possible humor, accusing herself of absurdity.

For Pearce the spectacle of this act came as an omen, almost as a justification. As Sydney shed her clothes, the resentment he had lodged in them shed itself from his shaky mind. As she removed her jacket and skirt, as she unbuttoned and carefully hung her blouse, he speculated on the advisability of turning away. But fascination held him. The harsh shell of the woman: he wanted desperately to see it destroyed, eaten away, leaving beneath it a creature he could cope with. He saw her hesitate, her hands upon her slip. She raised it and hung it neatly on a hook.

Pearce was shocked to see how thin she was in her underclothes. Her legs and arms were like a puppet's, pale spindles that worked quickly and delicately in their sockets. The pinched bones across her chest and her little stick-like ribs were startling. The frame showed strong and incorruptible; the body had wasted away.

He watched as she unfolded her pajamas, as she began to remove her underclothes; but her hands, fumbling behind her back for the catch, would not cooperate. She hurried at last to the light switch, and in the ensuing darkness found comfort.

In bed their isolation remained unrelieved by words. The bed was barely large enough for them to keep apart, and yet their separation was not difficult to maintain. Pearce fell easily asleep, while Sydney rocked herself slowly to sleep with mingled indignation and self-reproach.

At some unknown hour in the silence of the night, Pearce awoke, trembling, his body coated in hot sweat. His bones ached, desiring to move, but as he moved the cold air stung him unbearably. He lay awake against his will, bitterly aware of the wasted minutes, and of that oppressive fever that choked off his daily fulfillment in times of waking as well as sleeping. The face and body of his wife, as he had known her, drifted elusively before his mind's eye, forever unrealizable. The image passed from vagueness to further depths of vagueness, into obscurity. Totally unaware of the shadow-wife beside him, he slept.

In the morning they drove still further west, into the heart of Brittany, and Pearce found a measure of joy in the difficulties of driving. It was cold. On the road, in all spots not warmed by the sun, a veneer of ice slicked down the gravel, sometimes for distances of over half a mile, and as these were often difficult to see beforehand, and difficult to manage when seen, Pearce bent all his efforts to eliminate the insistent, incipient skids.

Sydney, whose clothes caught again today, like a dexterously managed shield, the many points of his hostility, sat fearless and inviolate in the front seat, intent upon the landscape. The brilliant greens of the fields, startling at this time of winter, gave the dominant note to the endlessly changing arrangement of shapes. Everything revolved in great circles on each side, the points of pivot fixed at the horizon, and everywhere the unbelievably green grass gave promise of spring. Yet along the borders of all the fields sprouted lines of weird, monstrous oaks, whose branches had been cut for firewood; they stood about in nakedness, mere black trunks covered with great bulbous knots. Distorted, limbless counterfeits, they suggested in the midst of the undying green another planet, ruined and tortured.

At times the road would sink between two walls of turf, heaved up on each side, and the landscape would disappear altogether, leaving the two travelers with a renewed consciousness of each other's presence and of the tension between them. Once, emerging from such a valley onto a plain where the road was free on both sides, the automobile began to skid on ice that had been slightly moistened by the morning sun. Pearce steered into the skid, trying to reduce its effect. But just as it seemed under control, the car slipped suddenly to one side. Pearce held the wheel. The rear end of the car scudded completely around, and the car went off the road, its direction exactly reversed. The turning wheels caught the pebbles lining the side of the road, and the car lurched forward, as though in one unbroken maneuver, onto the road, heading in the opposite direction. Unstrung, Pearce brought the car gently and circumspectly to a stop after several hundred feet. Sydney's hands still clutched the door and seat, and only slowly did her eyes and mouth resume their former shapes. She and Pearce relaxed by degrees, grasping the fact, with difficulty, that no damage had been done, that they and the car had merely been swung around. After several moments, Pearce reversed the direction again, and they continued west.

They arrived at Pierre's home in the early afternoon. When they entered the small village near Carhaix they enquired the way and were told that they could hardly miss "the chateau" if they continued along and took the second turn on their left. The proper address turned out actually to be a chateau, small, but replete with towers and walls. In front of the main entrance a large exotic tree threw mossy branches of tendrils, like green torches, wavily up into the air. They were met at the door by a maidservant in a white Bretonne cap, who went to call Pierre's mother. When she arrived, Pearce introduced himself as a friend of Pierre's from Paris, an American. She seemed to recognize after a moment the name and nationality and said, "Ah, yes. Pierre has often mentioned you, and he has often said that you might come visit us some day. And moreover, if I am not mistaken," turning kindly to Sydney, she continued, "you are his wife."

Pearce started, but Sydney, to whom the words were addressed, hesitated imperceptibly and then agreed. "Yes, you are right. Is Pierre at home now?"

"No, but we expect him back for dinner. Come in, please."

They followed her inside, Sydney rapidly calculating the advantages that her fortuitous lie might bring them, and Pearce thoroughly baffled and outraged by the deception.

Pierre's mother was a tall, whispering woman, who delicately wrung her hands together when she talked. Her hands and wistful voice recalled calamities already befallen, and others yet to come, that would sadly resemble them.

Inside they sat and talked for a while, about the house, the village, the land. Pierre was hardly mentioned. Once, when Sydney pressed the point, they learned he was, at the moment, out for a ride, somewhere in the countryside on his motorcycle with "une amie".

Soon afterward they were shown to their room. Left alone in the padded silence, in a bedroom stitched and plump with brocades and pillows, Pearce wanted to cry out his indignation. Moved at last to a clear emotion, he nevertheless could not bring it to expression. The cruel discrepancy between Sydney's lie and the reality of his loss pained him. By what refined taste for mockery had she spoken, by what indelicate lust had she appropriated him? He was too proud, too victimized by his own past, a past inexplicable to Sydney, to speak. He lay down on the airy softness of the bed's coverlet, sinking into its comforting embrace. Disdaining to question her, he composed himself for sleep. Gradually he shut off from his mind all thoughts of the usurper.

While he napped, Sydney brooded over his remains.

Tea was served in the late afternoon, downstairs in the large dining room. When Pierre's father entered the room, he seemed to be blown in by the wind, a beaten phantom in stray, unmatched clothes, held together by a white scarf at the neck and a long black overcoat thrown capelike over his shoulders. Instantly, Pearce was reminded of his own father; he regarded the old man with unaccountable recognition.

As soon as the father had entered, his benevolent charm exorcized the incipient tensions of their conversation, and it was not until Sydney asked whether they had any other children besides Pierre that the gloom foreshadowed in the mother's face actually sank in upon them.

"We have had two others," she murmured, in controlled confessional, "but they are no longer with us. The first died early. He was the most promising. Handsome, strong, always in the best of health, and he was generous, you know, considerate. And very intelligent. He was killed while at the University, in a motorcycle accident. Yes.

"And our girl," she went on. "She is now a nun. She has taken the vows in a very strict order. She writes us once a year, at Christmas time. We are not allowed to see her. Yes. She also was very promising. She was very active, always excited, enthusiastic, especially for the outdoor life. Sports and camping, yes, I remember. You know, she was elected regional director of the Scout movement, a high honor, before she was twenty. She was always extremely popular. Then gradually she changed, she drew herself into herself. All the life went out of her, and we lost her."

The conversation, after this, sank irrecoverably. Sydney, greatly affected by this intrusion of suffering, but not so much out of sympathy with the mother's defeat as in dread of her own unleashed, unbounded enmity toward Pierre, compelled herself to inquire: "And Pierre, do not his religious tendencies alarm you?"

"Ah no, ah no, Thank God, he has none."

Afterwards, when she had taken her leave, a great change came over her husband. He seemed to shake himself loose, as though suddenly released from a cramping posture; a careless, almost sovenly abandon appeared in him, which gradually showed signs of becoming extravagant.

The immediate effect on Pearce was a renewed feeling of kinship with him. The conversation grew random, gay. Yet although he tried, Pearce could not shake off the persistent impression that the disorderly man before him was his own father. His fever had begun to take its toll on his senses now, but pleasantly. Exhilaration, like a draught of pure oxygen, spurred him. "Tell us about your family tree," he said.

"It is a strange tree," replied the father, "a mongrel. It stems originally from the Orient–though who can say? I think it must surely have begun in Eden and from there, of course, it may have spread all over the earth. In recent times, however, within the memory of history, it is known to have flourished in the East, thence transplanted perhaps by the guilty conscience of the West into this peculiarly Occidental soil that we call France, where, as you no doubt noticed upon your arrival at this house, it has taken root and grown marvelously well. Did you observe, as you came in, that is now taller than our house itself?"

Realizing his mistake, Pearce drew in his breath. Pierre's father, his red cheeks, glowing, threw off his coat with a shrug, revealing a suit in which all the pockets–side, front, and rear–displayed protruding handkerchiefs, as though the man himself were only a scarecrow built of rags, with the stuffing escaping at every vent. The resemblance to Pearce's father was so marked that Pearce became alarmed.

"When the *Tedeschi* marched from Deutschland, they were very impressed by our tree. They descended upon our house as if it had some unique attraction for the Nazi mentality and paused inevitably to admire our tree. They forced our family to live in the barn, throughout the Occupation, with the animals, while they lived here," and he waved one arm, "in this house. They often said they were going to cut the tree down, but no doubt they were afraid, for to speak frankly, it is really the Tree of Knowledge out there. But on account of its soft, rope-like branches, too weak to support anything but its own airy plumes, it is nicknamed *Le Désespoir des Singes*."

His eyes bulged. His two listeners sat entranced. "Perhaps Pierre will take you tomorrow to see the many bottomless pools and deep mine shafts, filled with water, in which the bodies of many *Tedeschi*, murdered by our people during the Occupation, lie liquidly rotting away."

Sydney fidgeted, shifted her eyes guiltily, as though in disobedience to a respected hypnotist, and sensed uncomfortably the terrible pressure, as in the furthest depths of the sea, of the house into which she had pushed her way. She felt justified. Life, existing under such pressure, seemed capable of complicity. Her rash daring seemed less rash under such conditions, and as Pierre's father continued to speak she sensed the sharpened beat of Pearce's dormant heart; she felt herself less and less the fool.

"Or perhaps," he went on, "a more pleasing diversion to you would be our cliffs, not far away, they can be reached in a morning's drive–the cliffs of Brittany. They overlook the sea, a straight drop down into the ocean. Many a mother has lost her son or daughter there in a high wind, for there is no protection–save human agility–on the path that skirts the edge. But on a nice day, if the atmospheric conditions are good, the cliffs are so high that one can actually see America, yes, the country and the city you came from" nodding swiftly at them, "New York, and the torch of the Statue of Liberty.

"You are both, I believe, from New York, or so Pierre has told us. We have heard much about you, and your sister too."

They both started. Where had he heard of Sydney? He had nodded at Sydney when he spoke, but Pearce spoke out before her quickly. "My sister-in law? You have heard of her?"

"Ah yes. Indeed yes. She is, my son has confided to me, the only woman he has ever taken with him for long rides on his motorcycle."

The image of his wife's death jumped into his eyes, and momentarily blinded, he groped for explanation.

In swift pretense Sydney replied, "Yes, I know."

Pacing about, the old man continued, "He was, unless I am mistaken, quite occupied until recently in teaching her various Yoga techniques; in particular, I believe, abdominal control and the art of meditation.

"Perhaps you would be interested to observe a demonstration of a light stage of trance," he said, discontinuing his pacing, and deftly taking up a stance on the floor, alongside the sofa, balancing on his haunches, his arms folded. He composed his face. "My son has been trying for a long time to teach me his own trance techniques, but I prefer my own. I have no doubt that his are better, more philosophically sound. But I was taught this method so long ago, years before Pierre was ever born, in Indo-China while I was stationed there, I am too old to follow my son's lead." His voice trailed off and the magic light in his eyes, that had so illuminated them during his preceding talk, faded.

After a moment during which Sydney and Pearce looked on horrified, he said in a small voice, "You may leave at any time. I will wake of my own accord later." Then in a voice that seemed hardly his own and devoid of significance, he directed them "not to mention Pierre's yoga practices to his mother. She knows and understands mine. She knows nothing of Pierre's" He stopped, as if searching for words, about to go on. But nothing more happened. It was as if a human gate had closed on the world. After a while it became evident that the father's consciousness had utterly escaped from the room. To what spheres it had fled, what shapes or utterances it was chasing in that void, the drying mask of his face gave no hint.

Sydney and Pearce stared alternately at each other and at the balanced corpse. Pearce had been struck dumb. The unwanted tissue of confused identity obstinately weaving its way around him, and the precipitous refugee before him, vanished beyond pursuit to nowhere, were so many blows aimed at his head. He reached about for support, the fever thickening his world. He turned to the door and left, going straight to the silence of his padded room where he lay down, taut and hot, on the bed.

Into his distempered confusion entered the image of his wife's death. The corpse he had never seen drew his weary senses, and he found himself, breathing hard, in the coffin with her. On the bed where his own body lay, it shook in paroxysms. In the coffin he lay still.

He had not, of course, seen the accident itself, when she had fallen off, her head upon a stone, in the last ceremony of discarded flesh. That grimace had been reserved to Pierre. Witness of her ignominious failure to go on living, Pierre had remained in Pearce's mind an untouchable. But Pearce himself, performer of her last rites, had in this indirect fashion experienced enough of death to harden all his extremities; even those inner parts that never directly touch the world had gelled; the intricate swirl of living had come to rest as a dumb, ponderous filling-up of interior space.

And now the fictitious, final image of his wife's body quickened him. It mastered him, focused the supreme attention of his soul, and drew him on into the questionable intimacy of the coffin, into a future and unsuspected ecstasy of violence.

As he lay thus culpable, in this first pains of his own fate, Sydney watched the unchanging features of the father's face. She waited for a long time, incredulous and impatient, scarcely admitting to herself that she was trying to out-wait him. At last she wandered outside, thickly bundled in warm clothes, into the garden and orchards that stretched extensively behind the chateau. The air was cold, and growing dark. She walked about, sitting here and there, plotting her stratagem. To face Pierre bluntly, as soon as they three were alone, was imperative. And with the truth. She had met before, in Paris, with similar confusions as to the identity of her sister and herself. Her investigations had uncovered little else besides this confusion and the incomprehensible circumstance that nobody had been able to locate any witnesses. Sydney considered this again. She considered facing Pierre in various ways, with or without Pearce. Perhaps the ultimate action, as she had suspected from the start, would have to be his. With darkness closing in her field of vision, she sat on a stone wall under the Monkey's Despair. Its elusive torches made an area of deeper shadow where she sat, and she tried momentarily to fathom the riddle of the two trees in Eden.

While Pearce upstairs on his bed passed from thoughts of his dead wife to grating remembrance of what he now had left of her: the family resemblance in the dried shell he knew as Sydney, and thence to sleep; Sydney's thoughts in turn passed from herself and Pearce to the remembrance of her lost sister as she had known and loved her. Her fingers moved cautiously across her knee as she recalled the contours of her sister's body, the full, firmly-strung flesh, soft yet charged with something of the dancer's tension, and roundness that on her small frame were full but light; and still the remembrance of her sister's face that she now sought, would not come to her. Ann's seriousness, that had often held her face intent and rapt as a listener, her lips quivering to share the speaker's meaning, had been in the nature of a double fate: she had been too prone to defeat, sensitive on all sides to another's unhappiness, so sensitive that her soul could be borrowed, for good or evil, and often not returned till damaged; but this singular fate had had its equivalent counterpart in the rush with which she leapt to meet impinging joy, whether beating on her senses from the natural world or in the intricate demands of human beings. Sydney recalled the excitement in Ann's voice and the skip in her walk as she had last seen her crossing a bridge beneath trees. Unsure, questioning herself, Ann had sought shelter in the rough bark of trees, in the harsh surfaces of giant rocks, and perhaps not so strangely, in the benevolence of men. Pure in love, she had been first to hate. Such heedless love for particular men and women transformed its bearer into victim. She had, in the end, become Pierre's victim. Too openly participant in his cunning needs, she had lost her feeling for the workings of the living process–in this feeling Sydney remembered her best, in her frank rejoicing in the sheer currents of life–and had fallen beneath Pierre's unfathomed treachery.

But Ann's face would not take shape in Sydney's mind. In all these webbed remembrances she still could not recapture the features she had once known.

*

They had to wait a long while that evening for Pierre to come. They had all gathered in the dining room: Sidney and Pearce, and Pierre's mother and father. For the father had reawakened from his trance shortly before Sydney had returned to the house. Pierre had been expected some time before dinner. By the time the hour for dinner had arrived and passed, his mother was genuinely upset. Sitting in one corner of the large room, the table set and laden with food, Pearce and Sydney grew tense as they watched the streaks and shadows on the mother's face, shifting as her head shifted slightly with the faintest night-noise, hearing in every faithless, betraying sound the distant approach of his motorcycle. When three-quarters of an hour had passed beyond the family's usual time for dinner, it became unbearably difficult for the guests to continue to witness the mother's condition. As she showed no desire that anyone should begin to eat before her son returned, Pearce and Sydney went upstairs to their room. They had not been there long before the roar of a motorcycle, loud even in the distance, slowly split the night. When the motor had sputtered to a stop in front of the house, Sydney stood by the window in their room, which overlooked the main entrance to the chateau, and guardedly watched the path. Although the walk was largely obscured by the plumes of the Tree of Knowledge, a small area was visible directly in front of the large door, and there, after a few moments, she saw in the poorly-lighted darkness two figures–a large, bulky figure in a helmet, short fur-edged jacket and pants tucked into boots; and a short, light figure, similarly dressed, but wearing a skirt. They passed under the portico, and Sydney went silently out onto the stair-landing to listen as they were let in. She heard nothing, however, beyond a few indistinguishable voices, male and female.

Only five people were present at dinner. Whomever Sydney had seen Pierre with did not, at any rate, eat with them. Pierre himself seemed to take it quite naturally that Peace and his "wife" should be guests to dinner. He greeted them pleasantly, if a little shyly, and conversed in controlled, reticent phrases. No mention was made of the accident, and Pearce found it more and more difficult to believe that his wife was dead and had died in the presence of this gently, slow-speaking man.

Pierre was strikingly large. His head especially was oversized and heavy; already, though he was only in his early thirties, his hair had begun to grey. A slight charming smile would sometimes light his features, yet timidly, and then sink back into his otherwise closed unseeing face. This heavy and rounded head, reminiscent of the huge stone heads of Buddha common in the Orient, rested on a huge frame. Yet despite his bulk, it was apparent from certain of his ways of gentle motion that Pierre was deceptively weak. Though not fat, he was not muscular. His heavy body rested where he sat or stood as if it had sunk slowly down through some thickening fluid and come to rest on floor or chair in ponderous and delicate equilibrium. When his arms moved, a fragile mechanism inside, as of threads and pulleys, seemed to give him his precarious energy. Sydney wondered how he was able to ride his motorcycle.

Dinner passed without incident in a round of dishes, proffered and accepted, and conversation that was polite and well-guided by Pierre's father. The father had suffered no visible effects from his late journey out of awareness. The mother, relieved by Pierre's return, played the role of gracious hostess in a manner that gave no hint of her recent misgivings: no word was uttered pertaining to Pierre's motorcycle expedition. Pearce, intent upon Pierre, in whom he could find no trace of discomfort at their meeting beyond a continual shyness that seemed integral to his nature, had recovered from his feverish sleep and was eager to participate in the reality of a cheerful meal. But reality seemed stubbornly denied to him. Again and again, by some disconcerting, freakish mental leap, it seemed to him that he was Pierre and Pierre was he. It was, he knew, absurd. Yet repeatedly Pearce found himself sitting inside Pierre and struggling violently to choke off a current of guilt for Ann's death that rose within him to condemn him. The meal, in any case, seemed to go on cheerfully. Several times it occurred to him that there was something bizarre in the very normality of the meal, as if they had all invested it with a genial quality, which it did not rightfully possess, by a mutual conspiracy of denied identities. But this thought just brushed his consciousness and, with a flick of his eyelids which seemed to set the image "right" again–of five diners partaking of nourishment and engaged in pleasant intercourse–the other image, of grotesque unspeakable specters busied in mutual cannibalism, vanished.

Once Pearce said, as he put down his glass of dry white wine, "I see, Pierre, you don't drink"

"No," Pierre replied, "I do not think I would like to, but in any case I cannot: it is bad for my heart. I have a weak heart. It doesn't interfere with my activities much, except in small things like drinking and in the fact that I cannot participate in strenuous physical activity. But certainly I have as a result not been obliged to perform military service." His tone was quiet, restrained.

Her face alert, Pierre's mother added, "I wish he wouldn't ride a motorcycle. It's so dangerous for his heart."

His father said, "Pierre's heart condition is a disappointment to me. I look back upon my military service with pleasure. It was a man's life. It was the happiest time I ever had."

Later on he reiterated his suggestion that Pierre should take his visitors to see the cliffs of Brittany the following morning, and it was agreed that the three of them would, if the weather was good, drive out there.

After dinner, as though by prearrangement, Sydney and Pearce were left alone in the parlor with Pierre. After some moments of silence during which Pierre's gentle smile came and went several times, Sydney brought herself to say abruptly, "What was your relationship with my sister?"

"I was her teacher," Pierre replied gravely.

Pearce turned uncomfortably, beseechingly, to Sydney. "All right, really," he said. He felt that it was he himself, and not Pierre, who was about to be drawn out.

Pierre sat stolidly, balanced on the edge of the sofa, regarding the others out of convex, unblinking eyes.

"What did you teach her?" Sydney questioned.

Pearce stood up, objecting. "We don't have to talk about that. This isn't the best moment to bring it up, is it?" Sensing the imminence of a sharp change in the atmosphere of the room, he exerted all his strength to prevent the past from falling in upon them.

Pierre put his thumbs together, and his hesitant smile, in no way offensive, returned to his long lips. "You want to know whether I murdered your sister," he said and drew in his breath. Pearce sat down again limply in his armchair. "I did not," Pierre continued. "However, I recognize that I had a part in her death. We all had a part in her death, you know, myself, you, and you. But whereas you two have been transformed by her death and are in that sense results of her death, I myself was the instrument, or rather, –" he paused, meditatively, his round eyes searching for a more precise definition, "the method: the process. And I am in no way changed."

A little surprised by the alacrity with which Pierre had divined her intention and entered into the thick of it, Sydney was nevertheless relieved. She felt it would now be simpler to advance.

"Do you know who I am?" she asked.

"You are this gentleman's wife," Pierre replied without hesitation.

"And whom did you kill?" she asked.

"Your sister," he said.

Pearce stiffened in his chair. This admission struck him from within. He suffered the vertigo of the waker, the cruel rush of light on the eyes of the newly-born. It was as if, in the difficult process begun by Sydney's arrival in Paris, of tearing the web from his heart, the first significant rip had just now been made.

As for Sydney, her horror at Pierre's facile admission was mild in comparison with her renewed relief: her stratagem had worked. In this battle of wits she had pitted her speed against Pierre's poise, and she had succeeded. In the midst of her success, however, she was confused: Pierre seemed actually not to know that the woman he had killed had been Pearce's wife.

"Do you realize," Pearce said, still trying desperately to turn from the unfaceable terror, "what you have just admitted?"

"Exactly," Pierre answered at once. "I said that I killed your wife's sister, in the sense in which I defined my role before. I was the process by which she was annihilated. In that sense, and in no other, I was her killer, and I am prepared to admit that and take the consequences. But if you choose to interpret my admission in a crass sense, as though I had murdered your sister-in-law, I must deny that I had any such relation to her death."

"Then you did not kill her?" Pearce muttered. His head had begun to pound with the quickened tempo of fever.

Pierre hesitated, searching for a definition. "I was responsible for her death," he said.

Under the strain, Pearce found it difficult to think. He felt directly, without being able to explain it to himself, that

Pierre's apparent admission was an accusation, or rather was an admission that included himself, Pearce, in its force. He struggled to focus his judgment.

Sydney, however, in no way put off by Pierre's qualification, took his words as a stark confirmation of the hunch that had carried her from Paris to Brittany. She proceeded carefully, repeating a question: "What did you teach my sister?"

"Discipline," he answered, "meditation, and death. The arts of life." His great head bent forward, and he closed his eyes. "She was the best pupil I have ever had. There was something in her nature, some unpracticed urge to discipline which I believe had previously run scattered and vindictive through her life, and which I was fortunately able to summon up and mold. That streak of discipline hardened. Had she not died, she would have triumphed immeasurably. Her death was my error: I tested her beyond the breaking point."

In his armchair Pearce trembled and asked, "What did you teach her, specifically, exactly what was it?"

"Abdominal control for one thing. Control of the voluntary musculature and to some degree of the autonomic muscles. We concentrated, as I say, in the abdomen and pelvic regions and were just advancing, when she died, into some progress with her parasympathetic nervous functions in those areas. Largely we used breathing techniques, and these were also employed for purposes of meditation. We had achieved remarkable success with unconscious control, under self-induced trance, of the voluntary muscles.

"In meditation, she was particularly strong. Yes, remarkably gifted. She would sit for hours, sometimes for nearly a day, in unbroken meditation. This is highly unusual for a beginning pupil. We often meditated together, sitting for many hours on the floor of my study, and sometimes she meditated alone while I checked her breathing and other physical controls. Afterwards we would occasionally verify the course and content of her meditation, examining the degree of recession of the levels of her consciousness. In these sessions she showed remarkable insight. Her delicacy of understanding, the accuracy with which she could define her striking loss of awareness and apply its content to future attempts at reduction, was very rewarding to me, her teacher. I grew quite fond of her, you know. She was a constant pleasure to me."

His eyeballs bulged under the still, closed lids. His knees jutted rigidly into the room. "She was an excellent pupil. She had, I am sure, achieved before her death a narrowing-down, a level of consciousness, a point of controlled thinking, that I feel justified in describing as genuinely non-discursive."

"And trips on the motorcycle," Sydney interposed ironically, "were those part of her training?" She was surprised to find herself in perfect command of herself, though her thoughts were acidly harsh and her body showed signs of trembling. Apparently her arduous effort at preparation had stood her in good stead.

Pierre, at her question, snapped remarkably to his feet, his legs unbending, and elevating his heavy body effortlessly, in a smooth, will-less motion. Afterwards he opened his eyes. "You must first understand the function of a motorcycle in my own discipline. Then you will understand her accident." He began to pace the floor in sure steps. "The motorcycle is a convenience, but it is all I have that serves my purpose. Any other machine would do, but it must be a *machine*–without a will, reasonably difficult to operate, and capable of rapid motion through space. The motorcycle has the additional advantage of requiring, especially in the trance-state, a high degree of balance–of swift sensitive adjustment to the changing conditions of momentum and gravity–in the regions of the pelvis and thighs, I often ride the machine while in a state of submerged, meditative awareness,–which is a special state of trance, not to be confused with deeper forms–ride it, as I say, on country roads. I prefer the night, because it is more difficult, but I have not as yet attempted driving through city streets in this state. While the corporal person is in swift motion through the three dimensions of space, you understand, the meditative mind remains stationary in thought, controlling at the same time the muscular adjustments and reflexes of the body under difficult and rapidly shifting physical conditions. This is the purpose to which I employ that mechanism.

"I was not, of course," he continued in even balanced paces across the carpet, "foolish enough to give your sister such a trial. That would have been preposterously difficult for a beginner. I did, however, allow her to ride, in gradually reduced levels of awareness, on the back seat of the machine while I drove it. At first we travelled only on country roads. The day she died was the first on which we rode through the city. Her balance was superb. She mastered the complex demands of the traffic. Stops and starts were no great problem to her. In fact, in that last sudden stop, the most urgent and dangerous of them all, in which a large truck passed in front of us,–in that unusually abrupt change of momentum, she retained perfect mastery of her body and came to rest in perfect coordination with the almost instantaneous stop of the machine. It was only afterwards that she fell off. What effect the demands of that sharp physical shock had had on her motionless psyche, I cannot say. At all events, immediately after we had come to a stop, she fell off sideways. Her body went limp, and she slipped off to the right in one continuous movement, striking her head on the curb."

He stood, still, in a corner of the room, his head next to an electric bulb in a wall-candlestick that threw his bent enlarged shadow-head on the wall and ceiling opposite. Pearce rocked mutely in his chair, a victim of the story. Fever suffused his brain. Sydney suffered the story to rouse a new premeditated contempt for Pierre, as she weighed his sins and computed her judgement.

Pierre continued, "The experiment had failed. Or so I thought at first. I stood there, in realization of my defeat, in a good deal of irritation, and trying to calculate the cause of the error. I felt, I should tell you, at least at first, as if she had betrayed me.

"Medical opinion, I suppose, would no doubt hold that her death was instantaneous upon the concussion to her skull. It remains however a possibility, in my opinion, that she was dead before she fell; that her death, in other words, was the direct cause of her relaxing of control and of her slipping off the machine. Now as a state of shock is not possible, at least in its usual form, in a state of trance, it is possible that the extraordinary degree of control necessitated by my sharp stop had plunged her into the ultimate recessive level—or rather point—of consciousness: namely, death. If that is so,—and I see no reason to doubt it in view of her unparalled talent in that area,–then she achieved, in her perfectly controlled death, what others achieve in death only once in many thousands of years. She achieved an eternal life, the true, the deathless death." He paused. "It is possible at least."

"Do you know," Sydney proceeded coldly, "that the woman you murdered was this man's wife?" She waved the crook of her elbow toward Pearce. "Do you know that I am his murdered wife's sister?"

Pierre stared at her briefly, then at Pearce for a few moments. He turned away. "I did not know," he replied. "Was her name not Ann?"

"It was!" Pearce shouted suddenly. He stood up. "She was my wife!"

"I did not know," Pierre repeated simply. "But I did not, in any case, murder her. I do not disclaim responsibility. But I did not, as you suggest, murder her. I consider that inasmuch as she engaged of her own accord to take lessons from me, and inasmuch as my disciplines were never forced upon her but voluntarily participated in, I am no more responsible in a causal sense–" and here he walked gravely up to Pearce, "than you."

Pearce was tempted to push him down, for the precarious balance of his oversized body on his delicate legs was almost irresistible. But confused by the thrust of Pierre's hinted accusation, he hesitated.

While he hesitated Pierre spoke again. "I do not know," he said, "whether you believe in the transmigration of souls. Many people do. I do." He turned away. "If I am wrong, and Ann did not achieve the ultimate plunge into eternal Life, she is perhaps still alive in this world. Perhaps the thought can comfort you. I don't know.

"Is there anything else I can tell you?" he added.

"No," Sydney answered. "I think not."

Pearce stood in silence, shaken.

Pierre turned to leave. Sydney said, "Shall we go tomorrow, as your father suggested, on that trip?"

"I should like to," Pierre replied, a touch of his quiet smile returning hesitantly, but with pleasure, to his heavy features. "I think you have not understood. Perhaps I could explain further."

"Perhaps," she said.

"Ah, yes. I hope so. Good night." He stalked massively from the room and shut the door.

Upstairs in their room Sydney consulted her map again, as she had done the night before, estimating the distance to the tip of Brittany, while Pearce, nearly exhausted, went to wash in the bathroom. What bothered her most was the unexplained presence in the chateau of another person. She had meant to ask Pierre directly, but had forgotten. Was it, she asked herself, another of Pierre's pupils? "Une amie." The thought was frightening. Was there another woman being conducted half-alive on these nightmare journeys? She thought of that skirted figure as she had seen it enter the house with Pierre, and wondered suddenly if all the circumstances of her sister's death could have been a lie–a monstrous experiment of Pierre's. The thought was irresistible. Perhaps her sister was not dead; perhaps the woman she had seen had been her sister. Hate, fiercer than before, welled up in her against Pierre.

Knowing Pierre, the idea seemed possible. But fantastic. She dismissed it. It was too blinding.

When Pearce returned, she left, and he began to undress for bed. His mind was steadier now that the trial was over, more whole, though not by any means clearer, than it had been earlier that evening. The undefined issue of Pierre's guilt still oppressed his movements. Admittedly not comprehending all of Pierre's explanation–or had it been, he thought, an apology?–he felt nevertheless obliged to decide his guilt. Anger welled up in him every few seconds, only to sink bewildered, unfaced by any target. Unwanted questions demanded answers. Were he and Pierre victim and torturer, distinct and seperable, or had they been impossibly confused by an accident of birth? Twins, perhaps, of a careless sire, they might well have been spawned, he shakily saw, in a single lust, soul to soul, tracking each other down to the final blood sacrifice. Implicated in Pierre's offering, he could not bring himself to strike, as Cain struck Abel, merely because his brother's offering had proved more acceptable to God. Yet they seemed thrust now to the lip of the abyss, where judgment was necessary.

He hung his clothes on a chair, and thoughtfully unfolded his pajamas. He looked uncertainly about the room. Their talk with Pierre had ended strangely. Although the conversation had pointed unceasingly and terribly to his wife's death, the result had been paradoxically upsetting, a blow aimed from an unseen angle. In the wake of the mysterious workings of Pierre's mind, the previously unreal, impossible idea that Ann's supposed death was a fiction–of Pierre's making, aimed at some undisclosed, esoteric end of his–had for the first time become real, perhaps too real, too possible. Until now, the thought had been an untenable extravagance, based on despair and the fortuitous fact that there had been no witness. He had, it was true, never seen her body, but that had been a voluntary refusal. At least he had considered it so at the time. Perhaps, he decided, the idea was fantastic, but in view of Pierre's demonic subtlety, he clung now, without quite knowing why, to the possibility that his wife was still living, perhaps a partner in Pierre's conspiracy, perhaps with Pierre now in that very house.

The idea, however, was too intensely disturbing to be entertained for any length of time without confirmation. And even in that case, he reasoned, Pierre must have sinned immeasurably. In bed, cradled in the cushiony mattress and surrounded by quilts, Pearce demanded of himself what path he should take. Paralyzed, powerless, he swept his fevered eyes about the room unceasingly until Sydney returned, freshly washed, and shut the door. As he fixed his gaze on her, he felt sharply and surely that the barbs that hovered between them must first be blunted, and that he could achieve his quest–which was, after all, so intimately their quest–only if united with his wife's sister. That it was reserved to him to act, he clearly saw, but to act alone, without ally, would be an inglorious war whose foreseeable end would be the ravage of the wretched victor.

While he lay thus pondering his needs, she faced him with the question, "What are you going to do?"

"I'm going to think. Tomorrow we'll do something."

Relieved to hear him speak at all and resolved not to

repeat the foolish timidity of the previous night, she began to undress for bed, easily, calmly, without hesitation.

Watching her, Pearce felt again the same fascination, as the clear light revealed that beneath the casement of clothes in which she padded stealthily with many motives through the day, a woman walked. The small pile of clothes that grew at the edge of the bed uncovered an indubitable humanity that, thin as her flesh stretched, gave access and hope.

This time she did not hesitate at her slip and did not stop at her underclothes. Pearce was genuinely relieved by her unbroken motion, carried thus to nakedness, and yet again was shocked, and even more distressed this second time, by the piteous want of flesh–now that clothes were gone–to cover the framework of her bones. It grieved him to be witness to this poverty. Her face was and had always been so like his dead wife's that friends had often been unable to tell the sisters apart; yet the difference between Sydney's body and the clearly remembered body of his wife was so striking, despite the resemblance between their faces, that it held him, almost appalled him. He could not help remembering, although he struggled against it, that his dead wife's breasts had been more swelling–these before him were unsexed, unmothered–and that her hips had been more lush–these angular hips afforded no avenue. He squirmed to bear these thoughts. Yet he was comforted, as she hung up her clothes, as she found and put on her pajamas, by the unbridled honesty of his gaze, realizing that in this cold vision he had achieved an unhoped-for contact with the enemy.

She switched off the light and got into bed. Pearce, moved

despite himself and thus compelled to speak, said, "Good night."

"Good night," she said and rolled thoughtfully over on her side, searching for a face.

When, out of his peopled dreams, Pearce awoke again in the middle of that night, it was as if some commotion, protracted and clumsy, whether in his head or in his actual room and bed–he could not say which–had disturbed his sleep and gradually wakened him. When finally he awoke, the room was silent. In the muddy torpor of his half-sleep, in the confused meandering awareness that troubled his brain, battling the unwanted wakefulness that had thrust him unsuccessfully up out of the dark night, he turned. Had there been, his heavy thought demanded, some noise at the door? He realized dimly that someone had entered the room. There had been a struggle alongside him in the bed, summoning him from sleep. His fingers ran along the arm at his side. His response was immediate: the arm was unmistakably his wife's. Hovering in this thick moment, he embraced and kissed her. He did not for a moment question that it should be his wife. Under his fingertips he squeezed the inner parts of her arm: it was Ann's arm, soft and tense. Under the pressure of his hand the resilient ample flesh slid over her rib-case and slid in the small of her back and over her hips. The neat crest of her belly warmed his palm. Her long unending kiss held him; he sank and unwound between her scattered thighs in complete and fathomless union.

In the morning he rejoiced to see her head on his pillow. They sat up in bed together, with a rush of gladness, seized by the inexplicable panic of good fortune. Conspirators now in happiness, they rose, washed, and dressed, unable to disguise–yet anxious to do so–the most extreme, most profound amazement. Pearce cold not understand what had happened. Plausible hypotheses multiplied fertilely in his mind, and every other moment he found himself on the point of demanding an explanation. Realizing that she would certainly reveal the details of her reappearance as soon as she felt it to be right, nevertheless he had the utmost difficulty in restraining himself. It was only by virtue of his intense joy at her rediscovery that he managed to avoid pressing her for answers. In this elated, uncomprehending spirit, he heard her familiar laughter sing through all their busy love, and trembled with the anticipation of a final crime.

Who, in that miraculous reunion, had been the most intrepid conspirator, dissembled best, pilfered most–Pearce could not say. Too overjoyed to ponder, he watched Ann's small figure tramp gracefully across the room, watched her brush her hair with supple sweeps of the arm, watched her take the sun's hot blessing on her skin, watched her bound to the window in furious delight at the rich leafy spectacle, and especially at the flaming plumes and crusty branches and bark of the Tree of Knowledge.

She tiptoed at last to the mirror on the wall. She questioned it and received answer. Earnestly and gratefully, she regarded to the full her face, as a kinsman might once have probed the face of Lazarus risen from the tomb. Satisfied, she tiptoed away.

They went that morning, as they had planned, to see the cliffs of Brittany. Pierre led the way on his motorcycle and they followed behind in the car.

Pierre's mother had said, "Please, Pierre, you know it isn't goof for your heart. The doctor warned you against high places." Of all her family the least acquainted with shadow disciplines, she seemed to Pearce the most protracted sufferer.

But Pierre silenced her by a look directed at his father which caused the old man to say to her, comfortingly, "He rides well. He's getting stronger. Don't worry. He'll be back soon enough."

Pearce was gratified to observe that Pierre's mother and father were both struck by the change in his wife. They commented on it with mingled surprise, humor, and congratulation. They asked her again and again whether she really was the same woman they had dined with last night. They were pleased. They put it down to the change of air. As for Pierre himself, he only smiled. Carefully inscrutable, he made no comment. Perce's hatred swelled.

In the last few moments before they left, Pearce felt closer than ever to the old man. His appearance, bedraggled and out of joint, somehow suggested the meanderings of this soul, desultory and empty. Pearce was touched. Child of these wanderings, Pearce knew that his own spirit had as a result grown soft and colorless. Pierre, he saw, was rightfully the heir apparent to his father's house; yet how difficult it was to believe that the same loins had also quickened the tidy intricacies and stiff systems of Pierre! Were both sons forever condemned, he questioned himself now, both forever unredeemable?

Before they left, Pierre's father and mother said goodbye in a kindly fashion and asked them, when Pierre was out of earshot, to take care of him and see to it that he rode slowly.

On the way there, however, Pierre set the pace and it was

fast. In the car, Pearce, whose fever seemed to have vanished completely, tried to account for Sydney's disappearance. It was obvious that Pierre must by now have revealed the secret to her. But where was she? At all events, he was sure that Pierre was clever enough to have managed this last bit of juggling. He knew that he would soon be in a position to solve that matter, and for the moment he was content to dismiss it from his mind. He drove on, thinking of the cliffs ahead and gazing continuously at Ann, gladdened by her loved presence. He shared his attention between the road and her, taking even the difficult curves with one corner of his vision fixed upon her. Her small body set firmly against his side was a new life, created out of his rib, and he offered her now his love as she offered him hers, hammered, burnished, purified.

When they arrived at last at the cliffs, Pierre drove his motorcycle right out to the edge, skirting along it for several hundred feet and parking only a few feet from the drop. Pearce had to stop the car considerably farther back. He took Ann's hand and they ran out to meet Pierre. The shore was utterly desolate, neither tree nor person relieved the rocky prospect. The three of them gazed over the edge. Stretching out into the water ran a vast peninsula of broken rocks, and in huge separated mounds, isles of broken rock thrust up out of the sea. The ocean itself slapped these alien obstructions with its roaring, scattered arms, tearing its giant fingers to shreds. Directly before them, the cliff swung away in a smooth arc for a mile, cupped like a moon-crater around the bay that beat inaccessibly below them. The smooth rock at their feet fell hundreds of yards to the churning, rock-filled basin. Pearce turned to Ann and saw how strongly this jagged worlds had satisfied her inmost, chambered heart and set her tremulous face at peace. The wind blew eagerly, full of the salt spray.

A few moments later, they pushed Pierre over the edge. It was remarkable how much resistance he offered despite his feeble muscles. Pearce had almost begun to doubt Pierre's substainability, but now he saw his mistake. She pushed him first, and he turned, startled beyond belief. Pearce seized him at one and the two of them, against his straining muscles—which, in his upper legs and in the small of his back, may have been somewhat more developed than the rest—toppled his bulky figure into the deep air in an overwhelming alteration of his poise. They threw the motorcycle in after him. The ground was rock, and the wheels left no trace as it was rolled to the drop. As they stood there, looking over the edge for the now invisible traces of their crime, they seemed to be celebrants in a sacrificial rite in which the sacrifice had been torn from their own breasts and delivered up to the hungry ranting world.

Epithalamion

Fallout of leaves in spring,
Or that extra fresh egg
I'll bang open and find
A wrinkled midget hen
Inside, is what I'm afraid of,
And what little girls are made of,
Especially the spice.

I laid a girl on a couch.
But she only said ouch.

But if air carries the smell of
Salt, and a wife pulls off
Her sweater over a sea-limp
Breast, and the child in her womb
Is a fish, a milkloving fish
It's true, but only a breakfast
Away from the tide, and brained
To sail by catching the wind
In his diapers, and crawling the criss-
Cross waves on salt fours,
And wading out before he learns to swim,
And I'm the whale that spermed him,
Why do I fear the eggwhite
Splash of her wet
History, especially the spice?

I stood a girl on her head.
And so we were wed.

Round Robin

Everything's perfect. Something's wrong.
Sun on a postcard can't be mailed.
Addressees refuse delivery at seventy-four degrees.

Something's wrong. Everything's perfect.
My chair's chocolate, my back won't ache,
Insects are biting other insects and not me.
Everything's wrong. Something's perfect.
I'm mating with an ordinary Emperor butterfly while
A round robin stands still and still I can't stand it.

Yesterday I was inconsoloable. Nothing was wrong
Except the enslaved brutalized starving diseased billions.
My garden's weedless today, needless to say, what a day.

Summer '90

Not everyone is dying luckily. The list is short.
My mother, my father, the lawn. Not in that
Order but in some. An eggwhite cataract
Veils my father's one good eye.
He can see the word *war* in headlines.
Cabbies take him and his wheelchair to machines
That suck his blood and put it back,
Clean. Infrequently his wife, my mother,
Forgets my sister's husband's name,
Remembers to injure her skin with insulin,
Threatens to tune the piano with her cane,
Falls. It's insects, probably, eating that lawn.
Doesn't help hearing from my one big son
Out west, aggrieved because his car has died.
Or from his mother, who tells me she has married
The woman she loves. Outdoors.

Now that my second wife has given me my second
Son these first relations grow crueler.
How did I ever become my young wife's balding lover
Anyhow? Should I crow that I can rollerskate
My four-month-old so dazzled in his stroller
Over the clickety cracks in our sidewalk
Past that lawn, and make him laugh so loud,
So rackety loud, the insects stop eating it?
Not everyone's dying. Locally the list is short.

When the Oak Splits

When the oak splits, baby will spring and ants
Chisel my scrimshaw will. Glamorous lawnmowers
Clip feet to drive men mad after maidens do.
Okay, I enlisted in your service–but to see
Action abroad, not listen to rainbirds. I've flipped
Enough wheelbarrows of pulverized dirt
To raise the armies of your rhododendrons.
I don't care if it's high time I grew hoarse singing
Happy Birthday to You and *alle Menschen*. When
The oak splits, baby will winter and costs
Eat for three. There is no modest cake.
Only *zuppa inglese*, the country of my birth.

I kidnapped you there–fought against the alleys paved
With olives, the galleries reeling with Madonnas and gold,
The maps grateful for spilled wine, the eiderdown
Surf, the hotels disguised as mountainsides,
And the butter. So many beds too! You fought me to a standstill
In the bed of jugglers, the bed of bedrock, bed of flood and sand,
And me with the hat at the helm in the heat,
Steering for *spanikotiropita*.

Why not

Fight our way back, backpacking again, before the market
Crashes? We'll renew our passports, renew our marriage license,
Show it to the keeper of beds and this time he'll believe us.
We'll go to Sardinia, to poetry contests in the posh of night,
Where my folks will be waiting, kinder than ever,
While we go swimming naked in cold tidepools
So they can cluck and throw coins. Even if
Today's exchange rate's tipsy and tourists in terror,
Let's risk it, raid the treasury, see Rome again and die
Of agoraphobia under St. Peter's dome, see Venice and
Die from the Doge's prices, see picturesque Vernazza
And die climbing and counting 94 steps up
From the broken boats to our broken bed.
We can afford it there and hear, beyond the sea,
Lawnmowers, rainbirds, landscape of clamorous snowplows,
Earthquake of elms across the street and when the oak splits,
Baby will fall and labors of love make folks of us all.

Printed in the United States
By Bookmasters